Out of
LOVE for You

ANNE SCHRAFF

SADDLEBACK
EDUCATIONAL PUBLISHING

SADDLEBACK
EDUCATIONAL PUBLISHING
www.sdlback.com

ISBN-13: 978-1-61651-665-9
ISBN-10: 1-61651-665-8
eBook: 978-1-61247-359-8

Printed in Guangzhou, China
NOR/0413/CA21300733

17 16 15 14 13   2 3 4 5 6

CHAPTER ONE

Jaris Spain was walking onto the campus of Harriet Tubman High School with his girlfriend, Sereeta Prince. "Look," Jaris pointed. "Isn't that Vanessa with Trevor?"

Trevor Jenkins was Jaris's closest friend. A few months ago, Trevor and Vanessa Allen were very close, even though Trevor's mom was dead set against the girl. Vanessa dropped out of Tubman in tenth grade, and she hung with a bad crowd. Now Vanessa told Trevor she had turned over a new leaf, and they were together again. She was studying for her GED. She had a great new job. She promised Trevor that she would tell no more lies. She would be up

1

front with Trevor. Jaris was dubious, but for Trevor's sake he wished him luck.

"Yeah, that's her," Sereeta confirmed.

"Am I seeing things, Sereeta? Is Trevor giving her money? Is he peeling off bills for her?" Jaris asked.

"Yeah," Sereeta said, "he's going in his wallet and pulling out cash. Maybe she has some emergency or something."

"Trevor's been working like a dog at the Chicken Shack, always asking for more time too," Jaris commented. "I know he's helping his mom as much as he can. She's getting older. She just can't do those ten-hour shifts at the nursing home anymore. I hate to see Trevor handing his hard-earned cash over to Vanessa. She's supposed to be working at a good job now."

When Trevor told Jaris he was back with Vanessa, Jaris couldn't help but feel bad. When they were dating before, Vanessa's sister and her boyfriend, Bo, tricked Trevor. They got him to drive Bo to the drugstore, supposedly to buy cough syrup. Instead, Bo stole a lot of stuff from the store. He came running out, demanding that Trevor gun the engine and speed off. Trevor had been duped into driving a get-away car after a crime.

Jaris always believed Vanessa was in on that. He was not convinced that Vanessa had really changed. In Jaris's mind, Trevor had once again fallen into Vanessa's sticky spider's web. But Trevor was too much in love with her to see it.

Trevor had pleaded with Jaris not to diss Vanessa. Trevor now believed in her. He asked Jaris to give her some slack out of respect for their friendship. He told Jaris it would mean the world to him to have Jaris's support. And Jaris reluctantly gave it.

Now Jaris muttered, "Poor sucker, I think he's being had again." Vanessa tucked the money into her oversized purse, which Jaris figured cost a lot of money. Then she hurried away, like a thief escaping the scene of a crime. Vanessa had lied to Trevor in the past. Jaris recalled the old saying: "Fool me once, shame on you. Fool me twice, shame on me."

"It might be okay, Jaris," Sereeta reasoned. "She might pay him back. Sometimes people get a sudden problem, and they need money."

Jaris looked at Sereeta and smiled. She was so beautiful. He never tired of looking at her dark, velvet eyes, the honey-colored skin, the shiny curls framing her face. Sereeta had been through hard times herself. Her parents had divorced and remarried, and for a long time they ignored her. After a long struggle with alcohol, Sereeta's mom, Olivia Manley, was now at a rehab center trying to straighten out her life.

Jaris reached out and took Sereeta's soft little hand as they walked. "You bring out the best in me, girl," he told her. "Sometimes I feel that darkness that wants to surge over me and make me bitter and cynical. But you drive it back."

"I know that Trevor means a lot to you, Jaris," Sereeta said. "You guys have been more like brothers than friends, even when we were all kids. He's a really good guy. I care about him too. I don't want to see him get hurt. I mean, I know where you're coming from. I'm there too. But maybe Vanessa has learned her lesson. She's seventeen now. Maybe she's finally grown up."

Sereeta's thoughts turned to Trevor. She continued speaking. "Trevor hasn't ever had a real girlfriend before. His mom was pretty strict. She had those four boys to raise on her own, and she ran that family like a drill sergeant. She didn't even want them to date in high school." Mickey Jenkins's two eldest sons were now in the U.S. Army. Her middle son, Tommy, was in college. She had finally relented and given Trevor some space.

At lunchtime, Jaris and his friends went down the trail leading to the spot under the eucalyptus trees. That was where they usually gathered for lunch. Alonee Lennox and her boyfriend, Oliver Randall, were there. Sami was with Matson Malloy. Sami

Archer was a big, joyful girl with a heart big enough for everybody. The gang called itself Alonee's posse because Alonee had brought most of them together. Even as a little girl, she was the glue that held them together.

When Trevor appeared, he wasn't carrying a lunch. At one time, his mother packed hideous tuna fish sandwiches for him every day, and he ate them faithfully. Then she told him to buy what he liked. So he usually bought a tasty-looking sandwich from the machines, which he microwaved. Today, though, he was empty-handed.

"No lunch, dude?" Sami asked. Sami had a beautiful animated face and a full figure. Everybody loved her. In fact, the Tubman High kids once chose a school princess who best exemplified the virtue of the school's namesake, Harriet Tubman. Sami won in a landslide. If you needed a friend—even if you didn't deserve one— Sami was there.

"I'm not hungry," Trevor sighed. "I guess my stomach is upset or something."

Jaris had his suspicions. Vanessa appeared unexpectedly this morning and asked for money. Trevor gave her all he had, and now he couldn't afford lunch. Although Trevor was trim and athletic, Jaris couldn't remember a time when he wasn't hungry for lunch.

"My mama, she packed me two sandwiches this morning," Sami piped up. "I said to her, 'Mama, you want me to get so big that they'll want me at the circus?' She just laughs. She fixin' these two sandwiches with slices of roast turkey and tomato and lettuce. They got big juicy pickles and a lotta mayo with olive oil. Trevor, you got no lunch. How 'bout you do me a big favor and take one of these sandwiches off my hands, boy?"

Trevor's eyes widened when he saw the sandwich. "You sure you don't want it, Sami? I wouldn't want to take it away from you," Trevor said. "Uh, I'm not hungry, but it sure does look good, and if it's just going to waste . . ."

"Trevor," Sami assured him, "I sure would like that second sandwich, but it ain't good for me. Mama, she's big, and Daddy, he's bigger. But I'm wantin' to slim down a bit." Sami handed the sandwich to Trevor, "So here you go, boy. Take the sucka off my hands 'fore I fall into temptation." Sami grinned at Trevor. "You skinny, boy. You can use all these calories Mama packed in here."

Trevor took the sandwich and ate it with enthusiasm. Jaris's dark suspicions were confirmed. Trevor was hungry all right, but he gave his lunch money and whatever else was in his wallet to Vanessa. That really burned Jaris up, but he couldn't say anything.

"Man, Sami," Trevor declared, "this is one great sandwich. It's like on a scale of one to ten, a twelve. This sandwich makes the ones in the machines taste like nothin'. Your mama sure knows how to make a good sandwich, girl." He grinned and told her, "Thanks, Sami. I guess I was hungrier than I thought."

"You a growin' boy, dude," Sami replied. "You oughtn't to be skippin' lunch. Now in our house we can skip breakfast, lunch, and dinner. Still we got plenty fat on our bones."

Sereeta glanced at Jaris. She was thinking the same thing he was. Sami must have guessed at the truth too. In spite of what Sami said, she wasn't putting on weight. In fact, she'd lost over ten pounds during the summer, and her figure was looking great. She meant to eat that second sandwich. She gave it up because she thought Trevor needed it more.

When Trevor left early, Sami sounded worried. "That boy havin' money troubles or what?"

"He's working more hours than ever at the Chicken Shack," Jaris answered. "Tommy and Desmond are both helping their mother. So that's not a problem. Trevor helps her too. But with the boys all sending money her way, she's been able to work less and afford some decent clothes. They even got a new fridge."

Jaris was itching to mention the little scene he saw at the Harriet Tubman statue this morning—Trevor peeling off bills and giving them to Vanessa. But Jaris thought that would be underhanded. Trevor was his friend. He wasn't going to make him out a fool in front of their friends, even if he *was* being a fool. Still, if Trevor was as crazy about Vanessa as Jaris was about Sereeta, he could almost understand doing stupid things. When you acted out of love for somebody, reason often took a hike.

Jaris had wanted to date Sereeta so bad for a long time. He probably would have walked across the Grand Canyon on a wire if he could only have her in his life. The difference was that Sereeta was as beautiful on the inside as she was on the outside. Jaris feared Vanessa wasn't.

When Jaris was through with his classes that day, he went as usual to the parking lot to wait for Chelsea, his freshman sister. She was still grounded by their parents; so somebody needed to drive her home. Chelsea had acted stupidly, going for a hundred-mile-an-hour ride with two dopeheads. She lost her privileges to ride the bus, walk, or bike home. Jaris was hoping the restrictions would soon be lifted. He was tired of driving her.

Chelsea was always late in coming out. It was Friday, and Jaris just wanted to start enjoying the weekend. He leaned on his car, tapping his fingers impatiently on his rearview mirror. Today would be an even worse ordeal than usual. Chelsea wanted to take a quick shopping trip to the mall to buy some things she felt were absolutely necessary to her happiness. Jaris would have to stop at one of those hideous teen girl fashion outlets so that she could stroll giggling up and down the aisles looking at junk. Worse yet, she would not be alone. One or two of her hysterical friends would be with her.

Finally Chelsea appeared, along with Athena Edson and Falisha Colbert. "Oh Jaris!" Chelsea cried. "We *all* need tote bags. I mean, what we're carryin' now is *so* middle school. We just absolutely need new tote bags."

"It's dreadful to be carrying these creepy old totes we bought *months* ago," Athena agreed. "You hear what we're saying? I mean everybody is laughin' at us havin' cartoon characters on our totes. It's too babyish."

"Oh horror of horrors!" Jaris lamented, making sure they were all buckled in before he drove off.

Jaris headed onto the freeway, taking the ramp that led to the mall. He had come to loathe the mall. At least Chelsea and the other two wouldn't be trying on clothes. Picking out tote bags had to go pretty quickly, he hoped.

Jaris went into the teen store with the girls, feeling like an idiot. He would have preferred to sit outside. He'd seen a nice bench in front of the store under an artificial tree. A pleasant-looking old man was already there, but there'd have been plenty of room for Jaris. But Chelsea had grabbed her brother's hand and dragged him along. She chirped, "You gotta come with us. We need a guy's opinion. We don't want to get totes that Heston and Maurice are gonna think are lame." Heston and Maurice were in their group of friends.

"Man," Athena screamed, "look at all the totes! They go all the way to the ceiling!"

Jaris dropped his head to his chest. This was *not* going to be quicker than buying clothes.

"Some of them got 'Love' and 'Peace' on them," Chelsea squealed. "And such great colors!"

The three girls ran around the corner in search of even more exotic tote bags. Jaris heard Chelsea say, "Oh, hi Vanessa. You're not at the Ice House anymore, are you? We go there all the time, and I never see you."

13

Jaris stiffened. Vanessa, who was seventeen, came into this zoo? He looked around the corner to see Vanessa with her arms full of skinny jeans and tops. She saw Jaris and smiled, "Hey, Jaris," she called. "I need some cool clothes to go job hunting."

"Hi," Jaris replied coldly. "I thought you were working at the spa."

"Oh, they didn't treat me right," Vanessa told him. "I quit. I'm looking for another job now."

Jaris wondered what kind of a job she was looking for where skinny jeans and low-cut tops were appropriate. "You buying all that stuff, Vanessa?" he asked grimly. "You must have hit the lottery or something." Jaris knew where she got the money. Poor Trevor gave her all he had, including his lunch money.

"Oh, I'm not buying all these," Vanessa explained. "I'm just trying them on, and I'll get a couple. They're on sale. I mean, they're practically giving them away!" She took off toward the fitting rooms.

Jaris looked at the sales tags. The prices were reduced. Still, two pairs of jeans amounted to two days' pay for Trevor at the Chicken Shack. Anger simmered in Jaris's heart, but he couldn't say anything. That would just hurt Trevor.

Jaris stood waiting for his ordeal to end. Chelsea, Falisha, and Athena were laughing and screaming in the next aisle.

Vanessa emerged from the fitting room, clutching her purchases. Jaris remarked, "I understand you're working on your GED, Vanessa."

"What?" she responded with a blank look. Then she remembered. "Oh yeah, that. Sure." She flitted away to the checkout counter.

Jaris glared silently at Vanessa. She was lying to Trevor again. He was sure of it. She no more planned to get her GED than she was going to be an astronaut.

So, when he found Chelsea and her friends still involved in screeching discussions over the best tote bags, Jaris was in a

15

cranky mood. "Buy something and let's blow this joint," Jaris growled.

"Do you like this one?" Chelsea held up an electric blue tote with splotches of red and yellow.

"Beautiful," Jaris asserted. "That's the one. Take it, chili pepper. You got great taste, girl!" Mom was right, Jaris knew. He *was* getting more and more like Pop, especially when he was frustrated.

Falisha held up a yellow tote bag with peace signs all over it. "Do you like this one, Jaris?" she asked.

"It's you, Falisha," Jaris affirmed. "Beautiful!"

Athena had two tote bags, each bearing an obscure design. It was either an alien from a nasty planet or a vampire. Jaris said nothing more as he hurried the giggling trio to the cash register.

As they returned to the freeway, traffic was heavy. Jaris quietly cursed his fate. The car crept at a snail's pace back to the ramp leading to his neighborhood. Chelsea had to be dropped off first because of her curfew. And by the time he dropped Chelsea and Athena off, it was already five o'clock. He had to still get Falisha home, and she lived off the beaten track. When Jaris and Falisha were alone in the car, Falisha took her new tote out of the bag. "Are you sure," she asked Jaris, "you like my tote bag? There was another one I liked. Maybe I should have taken that one. It was green."

"No, no!" Jaris assured her. "Yellow is perfect for you, Falisha. It's really your color. Beautiful." Falisha didn't sense the darkness of Jaris's mood. She was too wrapped up in her choice of the tote bag.

In the backseat, Falisha fussed with her new tote and was quiet. Finally, she spoke.

"I'm very unhappy," Falisha declared.

"*What?*" Jaris asked. To himself, he groaned, "This is all I need right now. The angst of a fourteen-year-old."

"Yes," Falisha continued. "My mom is dating this really scarred man with one eye. She's trying to hide it from me, but I know

17

it's true. I know what's going on. She's dating Shadrach, that weird guy who helps the 'possums. I saw them kissing in the dark outside my bedroom window. I about died. They didn't know I saw them. How could my mom kiss *him*?"

"He's a wonderful man, Falisha," Jaris objected. "He's one of the good guys. You know how he got hurt? He was over there in Iraq. He got hurt fighting against the bad guys who want to hurt all of us—you too. He was fighting for you, Falisha. You should admire him. Where do you get off being so uppity about a wonderful hero? Is that a way to thank a man who gave so much?

"But Jaris," Falisha insisted, "he looks so scary."

"You'll get used to it. After a while you won't even notice his scars. 'Beauty is in the eye of the beholder,'" Jaris told her.

"What?" Falisha demanded.

"I learned that in Mr. Pippin's class," Jaris explained. "Someday you'll be in

18

Mr. Pippin's class. He was a fine teacher before his students drove him nuts." Jaris was fed up and tired. This day was not turning out well. "Falisha, where's your freakin' house?"

"Right there, the house on the corner," Falisha pointed.

Jaris swung into the driveway. "Bye Falisha," he intoned as she was getting out. "Don't forget your freakin' tote."

"See!" Falisha cried. "You *don't* like my tote bag!"

"No, no, I love it!" Jaris protested. "I was gonna steal it for myself, but you wouldn't let go of it." Jaris backed from the driveway and finally headed home. All he could think of was Trevor Jenkins going hungry because he gave all his money to Vanessa. Thank goodness Sami gave him one of her turkey sandwiches. Meanwhile, Vanessa was buying skinny jeans and tops with his money.

When Jaris got home, Mom was still at a faculty meeting, but Pop was home. Pop was in the kitchen, doing what he enjoyed a lot lately—cooking dinner. Pop's new hobby was good for the whole family. He was a great cook. And they weren't eating so many frozen dinners in cardboard boxes, like Mom relied on.

"Hi, Pop!" Jaris called. "Everything okay at the garage?"

"Going great!" Pop responded. "Business is up. . . . I'm doing chicken manicotti tonight."

Jaris put his books down on the end table in the living room. Then he went into the kitchen and got a glass of milk from the fridge.

"Pop, just between you and me, I'd like your input on something," Jaris asked.

"Shoot!" Pop replied as he put on his cook's apron.

"Trevor is hanging with that Vanessa Allen again," Jaris began. "You know they were together before, and she was sorta bad news. She almost got Trevor into big trouble. Her sister and her, they tricked Trevor into driving the sister's boyfriend to the drugstore. The boyfriend come running out with a lot of stolen stuff. He told Trevor to get away fast. It all happened in a second. It was too late when Trevor realized he was driving a getaway car. She lied and stuff later on. Trevor had the sense to dump her, but now they're back together."

"Don't like to hear that, Jaris," Pop commented. "A deal like that ain't funny. If she was part of that, Trevor is a fool to go with her again."

"It gets worse, Pop," Jaris continued. "She's milking him for money. At school this morning, Sereeta and I saw him giving her cash from his wallet. Then when lunchtime came around, Trevor didn't even have enough left to buy anything. Sami shared her lunch with him. Just now when I took Chelsea and her friends shopping, there was Vanessa lugging around a pile of new clothes. She told me she quit her latest job at the spa. But she can afford new clothes in this creepy teen fashion store. He also thinks she's getting her GED, but I know she isn't. I want to help Trevor. But how do I get through to him?"

Pop laughed sharply. "Boy, looks like he's gotta learn the hard way. He's gone on that chick. You diss her, he's gonna dump you before he dumps her."

"So I just watch him go over the cliff, Pop?" Jaris asked.

"Stay close to him, Jaris," Pop advised. "If she's gonna take him down, be there to help him when he falls. He's gonna need you more than ever then. Just be there."

CHAPTER TWO

When Chelsea and Falisha met in their algebra class for the first time as freshmen, they were thrilled by their teacher. His name was Spencer Tidwell, and he was really young, just two years out of college. He looked just like the handsome star of a new hit television series, *LA E.R.* Tyus Stamps, the young actor who played a doctor on the series, could have been Spencer Tidwell. Both were tall and slim with smoky dark eyes and full lips. Within the first three minutes of class, at least half the girls in algebra fell in love with Mr. Tidwell. But now, since they had been in his class for a while, the charm was wearing thin. Although still delightfully handsome,

Mr. Tidwell was a very tough teacher of a hard subject. At least for Chelsea and Falisha, learning algebra was like being blindfolded in a tunnel that twisted and turned on them.

Kanika Brewster was Chelsea's enemy since second grade. Kanika was not only cute, but she was a math whiz. One day, she stood outside class with her friend and protégé, Hana Ray. As Chelsea and Falisha went by, Kanika announced loudly, "I think the class is easy. It's a snap. Mr. Tidwell makes everything so clear, except if you're *really* stupid. Right, Chelsea?"

Chelsea turned her head away from Kanika.

"Mr. Tidwell makes algebra as clear as mud," Falisha Colbert groaned. Falisha's mother taught science, and she was good in most of her classes. Both Falisha and Chelsea were floundering in algebra.

"Won't your mom help you with your homework, Falisha?" Kanika asked mockingly. "Or is she too busy with her social life?" Kanika giggled and nudged Hana. Everybody knew Falisha's mom was dating Shadrach, the man who ran the opossum rescue program.

Falisha glared at Kanika with hatred.

The two girls walked away from Kanika and Hana.

"My mom teaches fourth grade," Chelsea told Falisha. "Math is easy in fourth grade. And I was even good at math in fourth grade."

The next day in class, Chelsea and Falisha got their corrected homework back. Both got Fs and a request to see Mr. Tidwell after class. Chelsea was mortified. It was the first F she ever got. Falisha was almost crying.

After class, the two girls stood at the young teacher's desk, their knees knocking. All thrilling comparisons between Mr. Tidwell and the actor Tyus Stamps had fled their minds. As Mr. Tidwell now towered over them and sternly scolded them, he was starting to look like Godzilla. "Apparently you girls haven't been studying." He pointed to the F papers in the girls' hands as if they were stinkbugs. "Those papers are terrible. Terrible!"

"I *do* study!" Chelsea croaked. "But it's so hard for me. I just don't get it."

"Algebra is so hard," Falisha wailed.

"Not at all," Mr. Tidwell objected. "It's easy once you understand it. Fortunately, we have a very good teaching assistant here at Tubman. He tutors math in our study lab. He's good at simplifying algebra. He comes three afternoons a week after school—Mondays, Wednesdays, and Fridays. Last year, he worked with several of my lowest-scoring students. He brought them all up to very acceptable levels."

The girls didn't know what was coming next. Were they supposed to volunteer for tutoring? Their question was soon answered.

"I'm sure he can do the same for you," Mr. Tidwell went on. "I'll sign you up, and you can start today, right after classes end. You'll be an hour late going home, but it'll be worth it."

Mr. Tidwell smiled a little, softening his face. But he still looked like Godzilla—a smiling Godzilla.

Later that day, at the break, Chelsea called Jaris from her cell phone. He was at the vending machine with Sereeta when he answered.

"Yeah, chili pepper, wassup?" he asked.

"I'm flunking algebra with that mean old Mr. Tidwell," Chelsea answered. "My only chance is going to this after-school tutor. So I'll be an hour late today and Wednesday and Friday. Is that okay, Jaris?"

Jaris looked at Sereeta. He and Sereeta were planning to spend a couple of hours at the beach after school today. He was anticipating that all day. He'd planned to drop Chelsea home as quickly as possible. Sereeta saw the agonized look on Jaris's face.

"Oh brother, now what?" Sereeta asked with a faint smile.

"More good news," Jaris replied. "Chelsea is gonna be an hour late going home 'cause she needs a math tutor."

Sereeta reached over and caressed Jaris's cheek. "It's okay, babe," she assured him. "The ocean'll still be there."

Jaris sighed and turned back to the phone.

"Okay, Chelsea," Jaris told her. "I'll see you then." He sighed deeply again and said to Sereeta, "This kid's got to be ungrounded pretty soon. This is makin' me nuts."

After their last class, Chelsea and Falisha trudged over to the homework lab for their math tutoring session.

"This won't work," Falisha declared. "I know it won't work. I've always been terrible in math. I struggled to learn how to multiply. Oh Chelsea, who invented algebra anyway? It must have been some nasty person who wanted to torture people. Why do they make us take it? What good is it? Most of the tutors are little old ladies who never taught anyway."

28

They reached the homework lab and opened the door. Falisha was the first to get a glimpse of the tutor. "Nooooo!" she gasped, drawing back, almost falling into Chelsea's arms. Chelsea saw him too then. Shadrach was sitting at the desk. Four other students were already there.

"I can't do it," Falisha wailed. "I can't! I can't!"

Chelsea grabbed Falisha's hand and dragged her along, whispering, "Don't be stupid, girl. We gotta pass algebra. This is our only chance. Tidwell will flunk us! Shadrach is nice. I bet he's a good teacher."

"Nooooo!" Falisha groaned, but Chelsea got her into the room.

"Hi, Mr. Shadrach," Chelsea greeted. "We really need help. Falisha and me flunked in Mr. Tidwell's class." Chelsea called Shadrach simply Shadrach when they were rescuing opossums. Now that he was acting as a teacher, she thought she should use a term of respect.

Shadrach smiled and said, "Pull up chairs, girls. Everybody here is a refugee from the algebra wars."

Falisha sank into her chair, a look of horror on her face. Not only was she failing algebra. Now her only hope lay in being helped by the one person in the world who turned her off the most.

Before long, the group grew to five girls and four boys.

"Okay, you guys," Shadrach began. "Let me be up front with you right away. There's a good reason I learned how to make algebra simple. I almost flunked it in school myself. Then I not only cracked algebra, but I went on to earn a minor in college math. So it can be done. Many brilliant math teachers can't connect with ordinary kids 'cause they *are* so bright. So leave it to a dummy like me to crack the code."

Shadrach smiled and added, "Mr. Tidwell is a fine teacher, but he can't understand people like us. We know what a nightmare algebra can be. But I beat it. I grabbed it. I took the terror out of it for me, and that's what I hope to do for you guys."

Everybody laughed, except Falisha. She sat there with a sullen look on her face. But Shadrach had everybody else in the palm of his hand. His scars and the patch over his eye didn't seem to bother anybody. Chelsea could see that Falisha looked puzzled about that. Falisha couldn't see how nobody else saw him as she did.

"Let's mount up and solve these equations, gang," Shadrach urged. "We're gonna learn how to read and write these equations."

After about fifteen minutes, Chelsea started saying, "Ohhhh! That's what I did wrong in the homework. Yeah!"

Even Falisha looked like a lightbulb was flickering on in her mind.

The hour went fast, and Chelsea turned to Shadrach, "Wow, I really learned so much. I still don't understand algebra, but I'm starting to get it a little bit."

Shadrach laughed. "It's a process, Chelsea. See you on Wednesday."

As they walked out, Chelsea remarked to Falisha, "Admit it, girl, he's gonna be a big help."

"I guess," Falisha admitted grudgingly. "He's sure a better teacher than Tidwell."

"Like he said," Chelsea noted, "people who had trouble with algebra themselves understand people like us."

"I'm not a dummy," Falisha sniffed.

"Well, when it comes to algebra, *I am*," Chelsea confessed.

The girls then split up. Falisha walked to her mother's classroom. They would go home together. Chelsea ran to Jaris's car. Sereeta was in the front seat. So Chelsea climbed in the back. "I'm sorry, you guys," Chelsea said. "I know I'm a big nuisance."

"No, it's okay," Jaris lied. "How was the tutor?"

"Jaris, you wouldn't guess in a million years who it was," Chelsea responded. "He's just amazing. He's so patient and stuff. He's much better than Mr. Tidwell. It's Shadrach!"

"Wow!" Jaris said. "That's pretty cool."

After Jaris dropped Chelsea home, he headed for the beach with Sereeta. She and Jaris had both brought their swimsuits. After Jaris parked, they rushed to change in the bathrooms. Then they sprinted down to the water. "Ohhh! It looks so good," Sereeta cried. "It's such a hot, muggy day. I hate the first days of school. It seems we always get a heat wave about now."

"Man, I've been dreamin' about this all day," Jaris yelled. "Babe, let's you and me run away to some tropical island. We'll spend all our time playing in the water. Then we'll sit under palm trees until the coconuts drop."

Sereeta laughed. "With my luck they'd drop on my head!" she laughed. She swam like a fish, diving into and out of the oncoming waves.

"Where'd you learn to swim so good?" Jaris asked her.

"Mom taught me," Sereeta explained. She brushed her hair back and wiped water from her eyes. "She's a good swimmer. We used to have lots of fun when I was little. We'd all go in the water—Mom, Dad, and me. Dad took a lot of movies of us. We looked like such a happy group."

Her eyes showed a tinge of sadness. "I don't like pictures anymore, Jaris. I'm never going to take pictures. Later on, you look at them, and they just make you sad how everything has changed."

They waded out of the surf, plodding against the undertow. When they came out of the water, Jaris grabbed his large beach towel and spread it on the sand. They lay on it. "This time of day, it's awesome," Sereeta commented.

"Yeah," Jaris agreed. "How's school going so far for you Sereeta? We've both been so busy I haven't even talked to you about school."

"Good," Sereeta replied. "I thought AP American History was gonna be a bear. But it's turning out to be fun."

"Yeah, Ms. McDowell liked my outline and that was a big relief," Jaris responded. "Mr. Myers is okay I guess."

"We always end up with strange English teachers," Sereeta noted with a smile. "Last year it was Mr. Pippin and now Myers. He's really trying to become a published book writer."

"Yeah," Jaris said. "I guess it's a tough business."

"When she was still talking to me," Sereeta said, "that's what Jasmine told me. She said Mr. Myers is really frustrated."

Sereeta reflected for a moment on what Jasmine had been through. Then she spoke. "Right now poor Jasmine is like a hermit. She runs from class to class and hardly looks at anybody. She kinda lost it when that homeless man got mad at her boyfriend, Marko. I guess Marko sent his shopping cart flying and the homeless guy hit Marko with the baseball bat. Jasmine was so sure one of the guys here at Tubman had done it. She ran around the school accusing everybody. She made such a fool of herself."

A concerned look came over Sereeta's face. "Then it turned out Marko shoved that guy's shopping cart, and it broke up in the ravine. Jasmine was like totally embarrassed. She was having such a good time playing the faithful girlfriend of poor, injured Marko. She was so sure that some dudes at Tubman had tried to take Marko out."

"When's Marko coming back to school?" Jaris asked.

"I guess pretty soon," Sereeta replied. "All the teachers gave him work to do at home. But he's got to get back into the swing of things. I expect to see him any day now."

They fell quiet for a while. The sun felt good after the brisk splash in the chilly surf. In a minute or so, Jaris asked Sereeta, "How's your mom doing at the rehab?"

Sereeta's mother, Olivia Manley, had been battling alcoholism for a long time.

Her second marriage, to Perry Manley, was in jeopardy. Her sister and brother-in-law took her to a rehab center in the hopes it would help her.

"Aunt Gayla went to see her," Sereeta answered. "She called me last night. Mom is doing well, but she hates it there. She's feeling like she's trapped and never coming home. Aunt Gayla convinced her to go with the program and just hang in there a little while longer. Then she can come home and be so much better. I think I'll be able to go visit Mom this weekend. Aunt Gayla would take me."

"I'd drive you, babe," Jaris volunteered quickly. "It's a nice drive. We could stop off somewhere and have something to eat."

"Oh, Jaris, it's a long drive," Sereeta protested. "You've got so much other stuff to do. You're always taking Chelsea around, and you've got homework and your job."

Lying next to Sereeta on the beach towel, Jaris now turned toward her. He was propped up on one elbow. "Babe, you think

37

I wouldn't gladly do that for you?" he asked. "I know your Aunt Gayla is staying at a motel up near the rehab center. She'd have to come all the way down here to pick you up. Then, afterwards, she'd have to bring you home and drop you at your grandmother's. We could just go up together and then come home. I don't work at the Chicken Shack on Saturday. Mom or Pop can just schlep Chelsea around where she needs to go."

Sereeta smiled a little. "It would be so good to be with you when I go there. I'm gonna be nervous, and you always make me feel better. You sure it wouldn't be too much trouble, Jaris?"

Jaris kissed Sereeta on her full, soft lips. Then he drew back and spoke to her softly. "Babe, that makes me sad. I mean, that you would think for a moment that anything I do for you is too much trouble. Don't you know how much I love you, girl? If you needed to go to Mars and if I knew I'd never make it back, I'd go with you. Don't you know that yet?"

Tears filled Sereeta's eyes. "Jaris," she sniffed in a shaky voice, "of all the good things that have ever happened in my life, you're the best."

CHAPTER THREE

On Saturday morning, Jaris picked up Sereeta at her grandmother's house in his Honda Civic. They headed for the rehab center.

As they drove, Jaris asked, "Have you talked to Perry Manley at all since your mom's in the hospital?" Sereeta had never had a good relationship with her stepfather. It didn't get any better when her mother's alcohol problems worsened.

"We talked briefly," Sereeta replied. "I think he sort of blames me for some of Mom's problems. He thinks I've added a lot of stress in her life by not liking him very much."

"That's ridiculous," Jaris snapped. "They wanted to send you off to some boarding school for your senior year. By moving in with your grandma, you got out of their way. That's what Manley wanted, right?"

"He told me he hasn't decided what he's going to do," Sereeta answered. "He hasn't filed for divorce yet. He said he still loves Mom. I hope that's true, but I don't know. I think he's waiting to see how she is when she comes out. I think he wants to keep the marriage going if Mom is, you know, healthy. Strangers are mostly taking care of the baby—nannies, day care people. I think Perry still hopes that they—him and Mom and Jake—could make it as a family."

"It'd be great if your mom comes out okay," Jaris remarked. "Maybe you guys could take some trips together, like the one you took with her to San Francisco."

"Yeah, that was so wonderful," Sereeta admitted. "It was the first time in ages that we were mother and daughter again in a good way. It was almost like I was a little girl again, out on the town with my mom. We had fun, like nothing bad had ever happened."

They drove through some crowded neighborhoods. People were out in their yards, raking leaves, mowing lawns, doing weekend chores. Then they drove through a wealthier area. The ranch houses were spaced farther apart, and some people had horses. In the distance were oak trees and soft lilac-colored hills. Then they were in a terrain of rolling hills, close to the rehab center.

"When we get there, do you want me to come in, Sereeta," Jaris asked. "Or should I wait in the car?"

"You come and stay in the waiting room, Jaris," Sereeta suggested. "I'll see how Mom is feeling. If she's okay with it, I'd like for you to come in and say hello. Mom's beginning to realize that you're always going to be somebody special in my life. I know she wants to become closer to you."

Sereeta put her hand on Jaris's. "Aunt Gayla says Mom is feeling so isolated. She sometimes feels like she's being punished, that she was sent away for being bad or something. When something bad happens to Mom, she sort of reverts to being a hurt little girl."

"I can understand she's feeling bad, Sereeta," Jaris noted. "Anybody would."

"You know, Jaris," Sereeta went on, "when I was little, my family seemed so perfect. I loved my mom and dad like you love your parents. Sometimes we'd all be playing at your house. Your pop would be yelling, and your mom would be yelling. I'd think, 'Poor Jaris, my parents never have big loud fights like that, I'm so lucky.'"

Jaris laughed. "They still yell, but they love each other a lot."

"I never thought anything terrible would happen in my house," Sereeta said forlornly. "Then, when they got divorced, I

43

felt like the sky had fallen down and crushed me. Looking back, I remember that they stopped laughing with each other. Dad wasn't home a lot. Mom would sit on the bed crying. But I never thought anything terrible would happen. Mom was the one who filed for divorce. But I don't think Dad was all that surprised or sad. I think he was done with Mom. He's married now to that other woman, and she has two boys. Dad seems happy. I don't think he misses his first marriage—or me."

Jaris felt bad to hear that. "No, Sereeta, I'm sure he misses you. But connecting with you would mean going back to a place he doesn't want to visit."

"Yeah," Sereeta replied, "but he cleaned house, got all new furniture. I was part of the old furniture."

Finally, they arrived at the rehab center. Jaris pulled into a circular driveway. It was a very beautiful facility—white stucco with a red tile roof, Spanish mission style. Flaming red bougainvillea plants were everywhere. It looked like a resort rather than a rehab place. You expected to see happy people walking around in sunglasses and holiday clothing or men and women in white shorts carrying tennis rackets. You expected to see people with golf bags.

But there was none of that. All Jaris could see from the outside was a young man walking beside an older woman. Jaris wondered which of them had come here to heal their demons. Was it the young man or the older woman? The woman was probably the young man's mother.

Jaris walked with Sereeta to the waiting room and sat down while she went to see her mother. The pleasant waiting room was filled with lush plants and glass-topped tables. A few magazines rested on the tables. The place reminded Jaris of a very good nursing home.

After about fifteen minutes, Sereeta returned. She was smiling a little.

"Mom would like to see you, Jaris," Sereeta said, reaching out and taking his hand. As they walked down the corridor to her mother, she clung to his hand.

Olivia Manley was not in her room but in a large solarium. She was sitting in a comfortable leather chair that overlooked a lovely blue-green swimming pool. She looked stunning in a pea green T-shirt and slacks.

Jaris thought how really bad he was about making conversation at a time like this and in a place like this. All the questions he had in his mind were not appropriate to ask. "Are you being helped, Mrs. Manley? . . . Do you think your problem with alcohol has been resolved? . . . Do you feel better now?"

Jaris kept it simple. "Hi, Mrs. Manley, how're you doin'?" His words made him feel like a fool. But they were the best he could do.

"I'm doing as well as can be expected, I guess," Mrs. Manley responded, a thin smile on her lips. "I'm so glad to see you, Jaris. Sereeta told me how gracious you were driving all the way up here and saving Gayla that long trip."

"I didn't mind it," Jaris asserted. "It's a pleasure driving with Sereeta." Jaris felt more like a fool. He felt his mouth trying to wrest itself into a smile. He thought he probably looked like an idiot to Mrs. Manley.

"So how is your senior year going, Jaris?" Olivia Manley asked. "You and Sereeta seniors! Where *did* the time go?"

"Senior year is good so far," Jaris replied.

"They're wonderful to me here," Mrs. Manley said. "The food is so good, and I go swimming down in the pool." She looked at Sereeta and smiled. "You remember, sweetie, when we'd spend most of the summers swimming?"

"Yeah, Mom," Sereeta answered. "I've loved the water ever since. Jaris and I went swimming in the bay the other day. I told him how you taught me how to swim."

"Yes," the woman said.

Mrs. Manley glanced from Sereeta to Jaris and back. Then she spoke. "I feel so strange here. I've never been in any sort of a hospital before. It *is* sort of a hospital. They're always checking my vital signs and making sure I'm taking my medication. And we have very good groups. We talk about, you know, different situations. I don't like to talk about my private life, but they tell me it's very good for me. They tell me I'm doing well and I can go home shortly."

"That's great, Mom," Sereeta responded. "Then maybe you and I can take another trip to San Francisco and see all the places we missed before."

"That would be lovely," Mrs. Manley affirmed.

Before long, the conversation petered out, and everyone felt it was time to go. Sereeta gave her mother a hug and a kiss. Jaris shook the woman's hand. "All the best to you, Mrs. Manley," he said.

Outside the solarium, Jaris and Sereeta walked back down the corridor and out of the building without saying anything. As they were walking outside, Sereeta commented, "She seems so sad."

"Yeah, well, who wouldn't be?" Jaris offered. "To be away from all your familiar surroundings. It's like when old folks go away to a nursing home. Even if it's for the best, they feel isolated and abandoned, I guess. She probably misses the baby too."

"Aunt Gayla told me she is making good progress," Sereeta noted.

"That's good," Jaris replied.

"Aunt Gayla says Mom is going to be taking medicine for depression even after she leaves here," Sereeta added. Talking about depression seemed to be difficult for Sereeta. "I guess a lot of people suffer from that. It's not any different from any other illness."

"That's true," Jaris agreed. A lot of people look at conditions like depression as a sign of mental illness, something to be ashamed of. Sereeta looked nervous talking about it with Jaris, as if he might think

Sereeta's mother was insane or something. "My pop's sister, Aunt Lita," Jaris told here, "she was treated for depression. Everything worked out fine. She's doin' great."

Sereeta turned her head sharply. "Really?" she asked.

"Yeah!" Jaris asserted. "She was just down all the time, and she wanted to be better. So she saw the doctor, and now she is better."

Sereeta got in the car, seeming relieved. "There's nothing to be ashamed of if you need a little help," she said.

"Course not, babe," Jaris assured her, starting the car. "But you know what we should be ashamed of? It'd be a shame if we don't stop at that restaurant just ahead and get some burgers. I'm starvin' to death right before your eyes."

Sereeta laughed. "I'm hungry too," she replied. "All of a sudden I want a big juicy burger with rich, creamy mayo, pickles, a juicy slice of tomato, lettuce, and a crisp slice of onion. And I don't care what it does to my breath. A tall cool soda too. I know the mega burger has about two thousand calories, but just now I don't care. I didn't do breakfast at all this morning 'cause I was so nervous about today. I thought if I ate anything I'd upchuck it."

"I didn't eat much breakfast either," Jaris noted, pulling into the burger joint. "Just some of those goofy-looking crispies that Mom buys for Chelsea. Man, they taste like sawdust."

At the counter, Jaris put in the order. "Two humongous burgers with all the fixings. And two sodas to wash the suckas down."

Sereeta was laughing when Jaris finished ordering.

After Jaris dropped off Sereeta at her grandmother's home, he went home himself. Pop was still working at the garage, but Mom and Chelsea were home.

"How did it go, honey?" Mom asked. "Poor Olivia. I bet she's like a little lost sheep."

"Yeah, she's sad," Jaris answered. "But she's doing well. She ought to be able to come home soon."

"Is her husband gonna divorce her?" Chelsea asked.

"We don't know, chili pepper," Jaris replied. "Maybe they can work things out."

"Why are people so stupid?" Chelsea declared indignantly. "He shouldn't be mad at his wife 'cause she's sick. Like Falisha, she didn't want to let Shadrach teach her algebra cause he's got some scars. It's not his fault he got hurt. I'm sure he'd like to look like our math teacher, Mr. Tidwell. He looks like that Tyus Stamps on *LA E.R.* But I like Shadrach much better than I like Mr. Tidwell, 'cause Shadrach is nice and kind. Mr. Tidwell is kinda stuck-up and mean, maybe 'cause he knows he looks like Tyus Stamps."

"I never heard of Tyus Stamps," Mom announced with a bewildered look on her face. "Is he a real person?"

"Mommm," Chelsea groaned, rolling her eyes. "He's just the hottest new star on TV. When he goes places, girls just scream and faint and stuff. I think he's cute too. But if he's anything like Mr. Tidwell, I don't like him either. Probably he's not."

"I'm not even forty," Mom continued, "and I feel like I'm living in an alternative universe. When I hear about the celebrities on TV, I haven't heard of ninety percent of them. This Tyus Stubbs could be a cartoon character for all I know."

"His name isn't Stubbs, Mom," Chelsea said in an annoyed voice. "It's Tyus Stamps. And you know who he's dating? They say he's started hanging with Na Sheena Craig. She's the hottest lead singer in the Blastin Caps."

"Who?" Mom asked. "Na Sheena Craig? Oh my gosh, it's worse than I thought. There are hundreds of famous people out there that I've never heard of. The world is passing me by."

Jaris was laughing. "Mom," Jaris chuckled, "before she went with the Blastin Caps, Na Sheena Craig was the lead singer for the Loopy Fruits."

"Jaris!" Chelsea exclaimed, giving him a poke. "She did *not* sing with the Loopy Fruits. You made that up. She sang with the Hearts of Darkness before the Blastin Caps stole her. You can see her all the time on YouTube."

"Let's run to YouTube right away, Mom, and try to catch her," Jaris suggested.

Pop came in the door then, covered with even more grease and grime than usual. All heads turned toward him.

"Me and the kid were run ragged today," he declared. "Every beater in town musta broke down and ended up at Spain's Auto Care. But the kid was stellar, Monie. You were right. You helped me pick a winner there."

"The kid" was Darnell Meredith, Pop's helper at his auto repair shop.

"Lorenzo," Mom asked, "have you ever heard of Tyus Stamps?"

Pop paused, a thoughtful look on his face. "No, does he live within fifty miles of here and drive a beater? 'Cause if he does, I probably stuck my head under his engine hood today. Who's this dude you're talkin' about, Monie? Don't tell me this is another punk the little girl dragged home?"

"No, no Pop," Jaris replied hastily. "He's going around with this Na Sheena Craig from the Loopy Fruits. He's got no time for Chelsea. She's way beneath his radar."

"Good!" Pop declared, tossing his filthy baseball cap into the dirty clothes basket. "Let the Loopy Fruits have the both of them, Tyus Stamps and this Na Sheena babe. From the sound of them, they deserve each other."

Mom, Jaris, and even Chelsea laugh hysterically. Pop looked at the three of them and noted, "Well, I'm glad somebody's happy. As for me, I'm takin' a shower. And I might be in there for a coupla days."

Jaris was in his room studying for English when he heard his ring tone. "Yeah?" he said. He was annoyed that someone was bothering him just when he was just making headway in understanding some obscure poem.

"Hey, Jaris." It was Tommy Jenkins, Trevor's brother.

"Oh hi, Tommy, wassup?" Jaris said.

"Man," Tommy started, "my brother is freakin' over this Vanessa babe. It's making me crazy too, man. She's after him to buy her some expensive pieces of jewelry and Trevor, he's searching everywhere for money. I'm tellin' you, Jaris, we gotta talk some sense into this fool before he goes off the deep end."

Tommy was talking quickly and excitedly. "Ma doesn't know what's goin' on. I don't want to trigger trouble between Trevor and Ma. But I'm tellin' you, if

Trevor thought he could get pearls for that chick, he'd dive to the bottom of the ocean. She's got him wrapped around her crooked little finger."

"Oh brother!" Jaris groaned. "I was afraid she was playing him, Tommy. I was afraid of that the minute he told me she was back in his life. She's a user. That's plain to anybody with a working brain. But she's the first cute chick ever came on to Trevor, and he's not thinking straight."

"Would you talk to him, Jaris?" Tommy pleaded. "I think he respects you more than anybody in the world. I love my little brother, and he loves me. But right now he's so hostile he won't give me the time of day. I told him what I thought of Vanessa Allen, and he turned on me like a tiger, man. He's screamin' at me about all these great chicks I know at college, but he ain't got nothin' goin'. I should mind my own business when he's finally found someone he loves and who loves him back."

"I'll sure try, Tommy," Jaris promised. "But don't count on it working. I've already kinda told Trevor what I think, and it didn't work. You try to come between a guy and his chick, you're gonna come out second best. I'll do my best, though, Tommy. I love the guy. He's my best friend. I don't want him played by some bad chick who couldn't care less about him. And that's all she is."

Jaris then decided to tell Tommy about what he witnessed. "Tommy, I saw Trevor at school the other day, handing her money. Then I ran into her buying a load of skinny jeans and tops at some stupid teenager store at the mall. She could hardly carry it all. She told me she didn't even have a job since she quit working at the spa."

"They fired her from that place, Jaris," Tommy responded. "She told Trevor she quit. But the truth was, she was flirting with all the customers and she was giving the place a bad name. Lissen dude, you're more of a brother to Trevor than I am. You've always been there for him. That's gotta count for something."

"I'll see him at school Monday," Jaris said. "I'll get some help from his other friends too. We all care a lot about Trevor. He's a good guy. Alonee and Sami can maybe get through to him. They're chicks, and they may be able to say stuff I couldn't. They know what Vanessa is. She's got her claws into Trevor for what she can get."

Jaris figured he'd tell Tommy everything. "Trevor, he told me she was gonna study for her GED. But then, when I mentioned that to her the other day, she looked at me with a real blank stare. That GED is the farthest thing from her mind. She's not about improving herself, man. She's all about using people to get what she wants."

"Just do your best, man," Tommy pleaded. "I'm so worried, I'm sick. I'm scared Trevor is so desperate to get her what she wants that he'll do something really stupid. We're both on the same page, Jaris. I can't let my little brother go down the drain. Mom worked like a dog to raise us. He's the only one left in danger, and we gotta pull him through until he's really a man."

When he ended the call, Jaris was in no mood to study Mr. Myer's obscure poetry.

CHAPTER FOUR

On Monday morning, Jaris saw Trevor at Harriet Tubman High School. "So, how's it comin' down, bro?" Jaris asked him.

"Dude," Trevor responded, "you're just the man I need to see." There was a maniacal gleam to his eyes. "Where can I get my hands on some serious coin?"

"Hey, wassup?" Jaris asked carefully. His heart was pounding, but he kept cool. "You in trouble or something?"

Jaris smiled, even though he didn't feel very happy. "You owe money to some bad dude who'll bust your kneecaps if you don't come up with the cash?"

"No, no!" Trevor objected. "But I need to buy a very special birthday gift, and I ain't got near enough money."

Jaris knew exactly what Trevor was talking about. He was just playing dumb as a strategy. He didn't want to come on too strong right away for fear of scaring Trevor off.

"Your ma havin' a birthday, man?" Jaris asked. "Don't worry about getting her something fancy. Your ma is the kind of a lady who appreciates the small things. She's pure gold, man. You just tell her that you love and appreciate her. Give her a big hug, and you're gonna make her day."

Trevor looked frustrated. Then he said slowly, "It ain't my ma's birthday. Vanessa, she's got a birthday comin' up. And she ain't getting' a party or nothin'. Her folks so mad at her for moving away they didn't even send her a card. I need to do something extra special for her. She's got her heart set on this necklace we saw in the store. She just went nuts over it and

I have to get it for her." Trevor looked distraught.

"Man," Jaris suggested, "Lawson's is having a jewelry sale. Half off some really nice things. There's some beautiful stuff for like fifteen-twenty dollars man. You could swing that. Why don't the two of you go over there and see what they got?" Jaris knew he wasn't getting anywhere, but he tried.

"Jaris," Trevor insisted indignantly, "I'm not gettin' my girl a gift from Lawson's! She saw this necklace in a good jewelry store. That's what she wants. It's a couple hundred dollars, man."

"Trev," Jaris replied. "Vanessa knows the kind of money you make at the Chicken Shack. She knows you help your ma. If she's any kind of a girl, she's gonna be embarrassed if you spend that much money on a gift for her. Sereeta wouldn't stand for me doing something like that. She'd take the jewelry back to the store and return my money. That's what she'd do. Dude, get real. I think Vanessa would be lots happier with some simpler gift, knowing you weren't going into debt for it."

In his heart Jaris didn't believe his own words. He thought Vanessa was just selfish enough to put pressure on any poor fool to get her the expensive gift she wanted. He thought Vanessa was a greedy user and she meant nothing but grief for Trevor. If she cared for the poor guy at all, she wouldn't drag him to a pricey store. She wouldn't whine about wanting a flashy piece of jewelry and put him on the spot.

"Jaris, you don't understand," Trevor said in a broken voice. "This girl hasn't had much good stuff in her life. She's always had to settle for third-rate stuff. For once she's gonna have the best, and I don't care what I have to do to get it for her." There was desperation in Trevor's voice.

"So," Jaris responded, his voice turning hard. "You want my suggestion, or you want a loan, dude? 'Cause, even though you're like a brother to me, I don't believe in loaning money to my friends. You know what they say. Loan money to a friend, and you're sure to lose the money *and* the friend."

Trevor obviously wasn't getting the message. Jaris took a different approach. "Look, Trev. My parents got a big mortgage on our house since Pop bought the garage. They're really scrimping, and I'm helping by buying all my own school stuff and clothes. My pop loves my mom more than his breath. But you know what he'll spend on her birthday? Twenty-five bucks, tops. If he spent a penny more, she'd be mad at him."

"No, dude, I don't want your money," Trevor answered. He hadn't heard a word Jaris said. "I just thought you might know where a guy could get some money fast."

"Trevor, lissen up," Jaris persisted. "Forget about the necklace. Tell Vanessa you can't afford it now—maybe later. Maybe for Christmas. You tellin' me she won't understand? What kinda chick is that you're hangin' with?"

Trevor's eyes turned even wilder. "You don't understand, Jaris! You're not like me. You're cool. You always attracted chicks. If you weren't with Sereeta, you could get another pretty chick. Nobody like Vanessa has ever liked me before. She's the only hot babe I ever had, and I'm not gonna disappoint her!" With that, Trevor turned and hurried off.

Jaris wanted to say more. But he knew that would just drive a bigger wedge between himself and his friend. Another plan took shape in his mind. He just heard something this morning from a guy who worked down at a coffee shop, Latte Lane. Vanessa Allen was hired there. Jaris thought that after school he'd go down there and talk to her. If she had an ounce of decency and feeling for Trevor, she'd let the guy off the hook about that stupid necklace.

Jaris was walking toward his first class when he saw Jasmine and Marko Lane walking hand in hand. It was Marko's first day back to school since he was whacked with a baseball bat. Jaris wondered whether Marko would say anything about the incident. Everybody at school had already heard the story. Marko had been out running in the dark when the homeless man's shopping cart got in his way. Marko shoved it, and it went flying into a ravine. The enraged homeless man struck Marko with the bat. For days after the attack, Marko and Jasmine spread a phony story around the campus. They were saying probably one or more of the guys at Tubman had hit him because they were jealous of him. Later, when the truth came out, she apologized. Marko didn't.

"Hey, Marko!" Jaris called out as pleasantly as he could, even though he despised Marko Lane. "You feeling better?"

Jasmine smiled and squeezed Marko's hand lovingly. "Marko's been through a lot," Jasmine replied. "He's really anxious to get back to school, though."

"Bet you and a lotta the others counted me out, huh Jaris?" Marko snorted with his usual swagger. "But it takes more than a baseball bat to finish off Marko Lane." Alonee Lennox and Sami Archer came along, and Marko turned to them, "You chicks didn't think you'd ever see me again around old Tubman High, right?" he challenged.

"Oh, I knew you'd be back, Marko," Sami chuckled. "Good Lord saw you comin', and He goes 'Uh-oh, ain't lettin' that dude in. He got a lot more repentin' to do before he's fit for here.' Devil was scared of you comin' there too. So I knew you'd be bouncing right back here some-time soon."

"You guys have any parties celebrating what happened to me?" Marko asked. The group was growing near the statue of Harriet Tubman in front of the school. It now included Oliver Randall, Alonee's boyfriend, Derrick Shaw, and Kevin Walker.

"We did," Jaris said sarcastically. "We had a mock funeral right out here by Harriet's statue for you, Marko."

"We built a bonfire and danced around it half the night," Oliver added.

Kevin Walker stood at the edge of the group, too bitter even to make jokes.

"You know," Marko declared, "there's been a lot of trash talkin' about me and what happened. They're saying I pushed that crazy old man's shopping cart into the ravine on purpose. Nothing like that happened. It was dark. All of a sudden I see this shopping cart, and I just gave it a push to get it outta my way. Who knew it'd go flying down Pequot and over the edge? I didn't think anything of it. When he tried to kill me with that baseball bat, I never dreamed he was the one who done it. I didn't even think I'd done anything to make the guy mad."

"Yeah," Kevin finally chimed in. "Who knew? Old guy shoulda been happy to see his shopping cart and all his worldly possessions going down into the ditch."

"Well," Marko asserted, "the thing is I was the victim of a vicious crime. But I'm strong and I'm back, better than ever."

Jasmine stood on her tiptoe and kissed Marko's cheek. Then the two of them strolled off with their arms around each other.

"Did you notice he never apologized for accusing all of us?" Jaris commented.

"You thought he would, dude?" Kevin snarled.

After classes, Jaris drove to Latte Lane, a little coffee shop tucked between a hair salon and a deli. There weren't many customers in the place. That didn't surprise Jaris. The store wasn't in a latte neighborhood. People didn't want to pay premium prices for their Joe around here. Jaris figured it wouldn't be long before the shop closed down and there was a for lease sign in the window. The neighborhood was full of empty places, and the only surviving businesses sold stuff cheap.

Inside the place, there were cozy little chairs and tables around the shop. But, except for one elderly man, nobody was sitting at them.

"Hey, Vanessa," Jaris greeted, climbing on a stool at the counter. "It's kinda hot today. I think I'll spring for an iced coffee, small."

"Sure, Jaris!" she responded flashing her dazzling smile. She was even prettier than Jaris remembered—and he liked her even less. She still had that dyed red hair.

"So, how's it going, Vanessa?" Jaris asked as he sipped his iced coffee. "Where you living now?"

"Me and a girlfriend got a tiny apartment," Vanessa replied.

"Hey girl, Trevor told me you're seventeen now," Jaris noted. "I'll be there pretty quick."

Vanessa smiled. "Trevor is so sweet."

"Yeah, he is," Jaris agreed. "He's probably my best friend. We go way back to toddler days. He always beat me on the hot wheels. I think the world of the guy."

"I think he's the nicest guy I ever went with," Vanessa commented.

"Trevor's mom, Mickey Jenkins," Jaris went on, "she raised four good boys. And she did it alone, without a husband. She worked like three shifts in a nursing home. She'd come home so tired she could hardly stand. I never knew a mom who worked harder for her boys."

"I know," Vanessa agreed. She had an uncomfortable look on her face, like she was wondering where this was going.

"Trevor is a hardworking guy too," Jaris continued. "We both work at the Chicken Shack. These hot days, man, it's no fun to be around frying chicken. It's a wonder we don't pass out. Trevor's trying to save money for college and help his ma out. He's heading for the community college like his brother. I admire him for that."

"Yeah," Vanessa responded, looking more sour by the minute.

"Vanessa," Jaris said, coming to the point, "Trevor has this really crazy idea. He's saying he has to buy you some really expensive necklace for your birthday. He thinks you won't like him if he doesn't buy it for you. But I'm tellin' him you're not the kind of a chick who likes a guy only for what she can get out of him. I mean, I know my girl loves me whether I take her out for a cheapo burger or to a fancy joint. I bet you're like that too, Vanessa, am I right?"

In truth, Jaris didn't think Vanessa was anything like that. But he thought he could shame her into changing her tune.

Vanessa looked upset. The tension was building in her eyes. Finally she smiled nervously and answered, "You know what, Jaris? Trevor wants to buy me that expensive necklace 'cause it'll make him feel like more of a man. I told him he didn't need to prove anything to me, but he insisted. He said he's got plenty money and not to worry. He told me he'd be the happiest guy in the world if he could clasp that necklace on me. I didn't want to argue with him 'cause that might have hurt his pride. The last thing I want to do is hurt his pride."

"Vanessa, take it from me," Jaris assured her. "Trevor doesn't have a lot of money. He's struggling, girl. He'd do anything to please you, but he plain can't afford that necklace. That necklace is the kind of thing guys in their twenties buy for their girlfriends. Kids like Trevor who're just seventeen and still in high school can't afford them. Vanessa, you need to get him off the hook. You need to tell him you don't want the necklace."

Vanessa's eyes hardened. It happened in a flash right before Jaris's gaze. Her soft, sweet girlish expression morphed into the look of a greedy opportunist. Jaris could see that she'd drive a guy to the wall to get what she wanted. Jaris had never liked Vanessa, but now he came close to hating her. She knew she had the power to make Trevor do whatever she wanted. He was a puppet, and she was pulling the strings.

Jaris decided to stop being a nice guy. He finished his iced coffee and leaned on the counter. He glared at Vanessa with the most menacing expression he could muster. "Lissen up, girl," Jaris snarled. "If you won't let Trevor off the hook out of love for him, then do it because he's got a lot of friends. You drive him to do something stupid 'cause you're greedy, his friends are gonna be real mad at you, starting with me. I love the guy like a brother. I've seen suckas like him go off the deep end over some worthless chick. Don't you be doing that to Trevor. Hear what I'm sayin'?"

Vanessa physically drew back, her eyes wide. "Jaris Spain, are you threatening me?" she demanded.

"Was I doing that?" Jaris asked in a mock innocent voice. "I thought I was just talking straight, girl. You think about what I said." With that, Jaris pushed away from the counter and walked out of the coffee shop.

Jaris hoped he'd at least shaken Vanessa and given her food for thought. Maybe, for now, she'd be satisfied with the cheaper jewelry at Lawson's.

75

The next day at school, Trevor seemed calmer. As he was climbing the hill to go to his afternoon classes, Jaris caught up to him. Jaris wondered whether Vanessa had said anything about Jaris coming to the coffee shop and talking tough. "How's it goin', man?" Jaris asked.

Trevor turned and smiled. But he didn't have his usual happy, open smile. His eyes were shadowed with worry, even though he wasn't as hyper as he'd been before. "Everything's good, Jaris," Trevor replied slowly. "Everything working out."

"That's good," Jaris said.

"I'm putting in for more hours at the Chicken Shack," Trevor added. "I hope Neal gives them to me. I'll be needing to make more money."

"You're already almost full-time, dude," Jaris told him. "You got to leave a little time for homework and stuff."

"What's important now is making money, man," Trevor insisted. "I can fit homework in at night, after I get home. I don't need a lot of sleep. Four hours is fine for me."

"Trevor, they say you need at least seven hours," Jaris advised. "You don't want to be falling asleep in class."

"I just need some more money," Trevor said, sounding a little like a zombie.

"Trevor," Jaris protested, "you need a good education. You want something more in life than working at places like the Chicken Shack, right? You need to save time for school."

"Yeah, yeah," Trevor mumble, breaking away from his friend.

Jaris thought that Vanessa Allen was affecting Trevor like a disease. Like a real bad case of the flu, she was draining his energy and confusing his thinking. She was making him cranky and clouding his judgment. Jaris hoped it wouldn't get even worse.

Jaris hurried to catch up to Trevor. "Dude, so you and Vanessa gonna celebrate her birthday Friday night?" he asked.

"Yeah," Trevor replied in a belligerent voice. "The big night. She's gonna be real happy. I'm seeing to that."

"Gift all wrapped, huh?" Jaris asked, hoping Trevor would confide in him. Maybe he and Vanessa had a talk, and she had insisted that he get her something cheaper.

"You bet," Trevor affirmed. "All wrapped at the store. I'm no good at ribbons and stuff. I'm all thumbs. It's gonna be the biggest night of Vanessa's life, man. Mine too. It's gonna be great."

Trevor stood there a moment, as if waiting for Jaris to say something. Then he turned and disappeared over the top of the hill.

Jaris wasn't sure what to think, but he didn't have high hopes. Trevor looked defiant, as though he was sticking to his plan to buy Vanessa the expensive necklace. In fact, he sounded like he'd already done it. But where did he get the money?

Jaris feared that Trevor borrowed the money from some sleazy outfit that would charge him horrendous interest. Or maybe he'd even gotten the money from some of the gangbangers. They'd loan you money all right. They'd also break your legs if you didn't pay them back with high interest the next month.

No legitimate outfit was going to loan a teenager a couple hundred dollars.

Jaris felt sick in the pit of his stomach. Trevor was hooked on this chick. He was like a poor dumb fish with a hook in its mouth. He was a doomed fish, slowly being reeled in to its end.

CHAPTER FIVE

Jaris walked to the Tubman parking lot to wait for his little sister, Chelsea. Chelsea had to ride home with Jaris since she'd been grounded for making some bad judgment calls. Driving her every day was a big nuisance for Jaris. But until their parents relaxed the rules, that was how it would be. Fourteen-year-old freshman Chelsea would be holding him up every day.

Jaris heard his ring tone and grabbed the phone, "Hey."

"Dude, it's me, Tommy," Tommy Jenkins said.

"I talked to Trevor," Jaris advised, "but I'm not so sure—"

Tommy broke into Jaris's words. "Man, it's bad. It's real bad. I can't believe what that freakin' idiot did!"

"Waddya sayin' man?" Jaris demanded, getting chills.

"Ma, she keeps cash in the steel box in the closet of her room," Tommy explained. "She always keeps about three hundred dollars in the box. Only me and Trevor know about it. She's always said if something really important happens and we need money fast, it's there. But we're not supposed to touch it except in an emergency. Ma keeps the box under her T-shirts and slacks. I seen Trevor go in Ma's room last night. He had no business bein' in there. So I asked him, and he said he had a headache and he's borrowing aspirin."

Tommy was silent for a moment. "Oh man! It never dawned on me what he was really doin' in there, Jaris. But then he borrowed my car and when he came home he had this ritzy package, with gold paper and ribbons. I just looked under his bed, and I

81

found the sales slip for the necklace. Jaris, he stole Ma's money to get that trashy chick the necklace!"

"You sure he took the money, man?" Jaris asked.

"I checked Ma's box," Tommy explained. "It's all gone but two twenties. She kept the money in twenties. There was always fifteen twenties in there. Now there's two."

Tommy's voice was shattered. "Lissen Jaris," he went on, "he'll be home from school in a few minutes. I promised to let him borrow my car to take Vanessa to that restaurant for her birthday. That's before I knew what he did. When he gets home, I'm grabbin' him by the scruff of the neck and draggin' him down to the jewelry store. He's gonna return the necklace and get Ma's money back. Jaris, I need help."

"You got it man," Jaris pledged. "I see my sister coming now. I'll drop her home and be over there in a few minutes. I'll be there with you, Tommy. It'd be a terrible thing if your ma knew what he'd done. She can't find that out. It'd break her heart."

Jaris's heart was pounding. Now he knew that's why Trevor was so desperate for more hours at the Chicken Shack. He wanted to repay the money he'd stolen as quickly as possible. But that wasn't the point. The point was he'd stolen from his own mother to please that rotten chick. Vanessa was taking his very soul!

Chelsea noticed something was wrong the minute she got in the car. "Wassup, Jaris? You okay?"

"Some trouble over at the Jenkins house, chili pepper," Jaris assured her. "It's okay, but I gotta drop you fast and get over there." He could hardly get his breath.

Jaris didn't know how Trevor would react when he and Tommy confronted him. Could they get him to return the necklace and get Ma's money back? Trevor was a good guy. He wasn't violent, but being with Vanessa Allen had twisted him badly.

When Jaris arrived at the Jenkins house, he saw Tommy and Trevor in the front yard, yelling at each other. Mickey Jenkins, their mother, was still at work at the nursing home. Jaris jumped from his Honda and hurried over. "Hey Trevor, you gotta do this. You gotta put your mother's money back," he shouted.

"I'm gonna put it back next week," Trevor insisted. "I got pay comin' from the Chicken Shack. I can borrow the rest from those joints that give payday loans. I swear I'll put it back in Ma's box."

"Nobody's gonna loan a punk kid like you money," Tommy snarled. "Lissen up, little brother, if you don't hand that box over with the necklace in it, I'll take it from you."

"You can't do this," Trevor almost screamed. "I promised Vanessa I'd give it to her tonight! She's been dreamin' about it for weeks."

"What if Ma looks in her box tonight and finds the money gone?" Tommy yelled.

"Waddya think she's gonna do? Her own son stealin' money she's been savin' up from a stinkin' job standin' on her feet all day, liftin' sick old people. How could you do that, man? How could you steal Ma's emergency money?"

"I didn't steal it," Trevor cried, "I borrowed it for a couple days. I'll put it back!"

Tommy grabbed Trevor by his shirt-front, "You're comin' downtown right now and getting' the money back for the necklace. It's happenin' right now, dude. Once we get Ma's money back in the box, you can borrow my car to take that witch to dinner if you want. But first you're returnin' the necklace and getting' Ma's money back." Tommy was shouting in Trevor's face.

Trevor was shaking with rage and anguish. He shook free of Tommy's grasp. "I'll get a cab for my date with Vanessa. I don't need your freakin' car." Trevor turned around, punching Tommy in the face. Tommy staggered backward, landing in the dirt. He scrambled to his feet and lunged at Trevor. Both boys were rolling in the dirt when Tommy was able to pin Trevor to the ground. Tommy shouted to Jaris. "Go in the house and get the necklace. It's in a gold box under Trevor's bed. The sales slip is there too. Get it all."

"Jaris," Trevor yelled, "you touch that necklace and we're finished, man."

Jaris sprinted in the house and found the gold box in the bag from the expensive jewelry store. The receipt was there too. He took everything back outside and saw that Tommy was getting the better of Trevor. Tommy was the stronger of the two. When he slapped Trevor hard in the face, Trevor seemed stunned and helpless.

Tommy dragged Trevor to Jaris's Honda and shoved him into the back seat. Jaris got behind the wheel, and they took off.

"You can't do this to me!" Trevor was almost sobbing.

"You wanna bet, fool?" Tommy snarled. "You know what Ma would do if I told her what you did. She'd knot up a bunch of wet towels and beat you until your face was twice its size. And you'd have it comin' too. You think Desmond or Junior ever stole from Ma? You think I ever did? I'd go through fire before takin' a penny from that woman. She sweats blood to make her money, and you're some kind of lowlife to take it."

"I told you," Trevor insisted. "I'll put it back. I'll put every penny back."

"Shut up, fool," Tommy sneered. "I feel like hog-tyin' you and hangin' you from the cottonwood tree. Then I'd take a broom and whack you till you can't talk no more."

At the jewelry store, the three boys went in together. Trevor returned the necklace and got his money back—two hundred and seventy-five dollars. He had stolen two hundred and sixty from his mother's box. The rest—fifteen dollars—was his own money.

"I'll never forgive you for doin' this to me, Tommy," Trevor declared. "You neither, Jaris. I thought you were my friend, but you're not. You're a dirty backstabber. And you ain't no brother of mine no more, Tommy."

When they got back to the house, Tommy took Trevor's wallet right out of his pocket. Tommy went inside and returned the money to Ma's steel box. It once again had three hundred dollars in it. He left the extra fifteen dollars in the wallet.

Then he went back into the hall, where Trevor was waiting. Tommy grabbed Trevor's shoulders and gave him a shake, "Lissen up, fool," he hissed. "You ever steal from Ma again, I swear to you I will personally call the cops and have you arrested. I mean it, boy. Stealin' from Ma is no different than stealin' from a store. Just 'cause she's our ma don't mean she's got no rights to her own money."

Tommy gave his brother another hard shake. "Ma told us where the money was. She trusted us. She said we could go to that poor little pile of bills if we were in desperate need. But you took it to buy a necklace for some no-good worthless chick like Vanessa Allen. You make me wanna puke, boy."

Trevor was sobbing. Tommy let go of his brother's shoulders and shoved him backward so hard that Trevor almost fell down. Tommy flipped the wallet back to Trevor, but it fell, open, on the floor. Jaris picked it up and noticed a picture in it. In the picture, Vanessa and another girl were standing in front of a bright green stucco building. Jaris knew where that was. The color was so wild, he'd noticed it a couple of times.

Trevor snatched the wallet from Jaris's hand and stuffed it into his pocket.

"The money in there is yours, fool," Tommy sneered. "The rest belongs to Ma."

Trevor wheeled around and took off, running outside and down the street—fast. He soon disappeared in the gathering dusk.

"Thanks, Jaris," Tommy said in an exhausted voice. "I couldn't have gotten it done without you. I needed you to get the necklace and help me get it down to the jewelry store. I couldn't have driven with that fool in the car fighting me."

Jaris nodded. "I feel really bad that this happened. Trevor is such a good friend. Man, I just feel so bad."

"You think I don't feel bad?" Tommy responded with a shudder. "He's my little brother. I've seen Ma in there countin' the money, so glad we had some in an emergency. He didn't just take a twenty. That would have been bad enough. He almost cleaned her out. And for what? For that freakin' trick. How do you think it makes me feel that my little brother would do that?" Tommy was shaking his head from side to side. He looked like he was about to cry.

"It's awful," Jaris remarked.

"Yeah, Ma never locked her door against us kids," Tommy stated. "That's how much she trusts us. Lotta parents lock their rooms. You know what it woulda done to her if she found out? Only thing keeping

Ma together is believing she's raised good boys."

"Tommy," Jaris pledged, "I swear to you that what happened here tonight stays here. I won't talk about it to anybody, not even to my family."

"I hear ya, Jaris," Tommy replied. "I appreciate that from the bottom of my heart. Maybe Trevor'll learn somethin' from what happened. Maybe he'll come to his senses and be the good person he is down deep."

"I think so, Tommy," Jaris assured him, "I really do. This wasn't who he is. It just isn't. Next time I see Trevor, I won't even mention this. I won't ever bring it up."

"Good," Tommy said. "I won't either."

The boys clasped hands and then hugged each other. Jaris turned and walked back to his car. He felt deeply sad as he drove home.

Nothing this serious had ever happened in Jaris's long friendship with Trevor. Jaris was afraid that Trevor was so humiliated tonight that he'd never want to look at Jaris again. Still, Jaris had to help Tommy.

Jaris could forgive what Trevor had done. It was a case of a good guy losing his mind over a hot bad chick. Temporary insanity. But could Trevor forgive how he had been humiliated by his brother and his best friend?

Jaris had to balance the risks when he went to the Jenkins house tonight. But he was sure of one thing. Mickey Jenkins could not have survived knowing that her son—her baby—had robbed her. Protecting her was why he went to help Tommy. She had to be prevented from finding out at all costs. Her feelings had to be spared. She would never look at Trevor in the same way again.

Above all else, Mickey Jenkins had to be spared losing the one thing she treasured more than life itself. She had to be allowed to keep her belief that she had raised four good boys. She had struggled all her life, working like a dog. She went without any of the luxuries or even many of the necessities that most people have. Through it all, she could go to the Holiness Awakening Church on Sunday and sing with a happy heart. You'd often hear her say, "Lord, you gave me four boys, and I didn't have a man to help me. But I done good, Lord 'cause I raised them all right. Now they're good boys."

Jaris was sad at what he had to witness tonight, but he did not regret what he did. He had to do what he did.

When Jaris came into his house, Chelsea asked him, "Hey Jare, everything okay at the Jenkins house?"

"Yeah, chili pepper, just a little dustup," Jaris answered. "I was helping them figure stuff out."

Jaris dreaded the next day at school. He dreaded seeing Trevor. Or would Trevor even go to Tubman High anymore? Maybe he was so messed up that he'd drop out of school, as Vanessa had done. It meant so much to

Trevor to be treated like a man, and Tommy and Jaris had treated him like a bad child.

Jaris brought Chelsea to school. When she went off, he walked reluctantly past the statue of Harriet Tubman. Usually somebody came along, and he exchanged a few words before heading for the first class.

Often Alonee or Kevin came along, but not today. Jaris spotted Trevor Jenkins walking toward the statue. Jaris felt like ducking out of sight. He wasn't up to facing Trevor. But he stood there by Harriet Tubman. He was hoping to absorb some of her courage just by standing near her statue. He thought he might as well get it over with. If Trevor cursed him, Jaris might as well know the score.

Trevor seemed to slow down when he spotted Jaris. For a second, he looked as though he might turn in another direction. He'd have to enter the Tubman campus by the long way, just to avoid meeting Jaris.

But then Trevor turned again and began walking directly toward Jaris. When Trevor got close, Jaris greeted him. "Hey man, wassup?"

Trevor stood there staring at Jaris. Then he spoke slowly. "I woulda given the money back."

"What money?" Jaris asked.

"You know—" Trevor began. He didn't look angry, as Jaris expected him to be. He looked beaten, sad, and frightened.

"Test in English today," Jaris noted. "Myers. Don't know where that dude is coming from. I hope you read those poems by Arna Bontemps. They won the Pushkin Prize, whatever that is."

The two boys stood there then, looking at each other. Trevor took a step forward, and so did Jaris. They hugged each other and then wordlessly split, going to their separate classes.

Jaris felt as though a great load had been lifted from his shoulders. He almost bounded into Ms. McDowell's AP American History class.

Marko Lane was there. While recuperating from his injuries, he had done a lot of reading and had prepared his outline. He was caught up on everything he missed. So there he was, smiling and looking around like a hero returned from the war.

His injury had turned out to be a mild concussion, and the laceration was healing well. The homeless man was too old and weak to deliver a really strong blow. But before Ms. McDowell arrived, he was regaling everyone with his harrowing hospital experiences. He told tales of the MRI and his time in the ICU, where he "hung between life and death." Marko claimed he looked "over the edge of eternity."

"Did your whole life pass before your eyes, Marko?" Oliver Randall asked, with a smirk.

"Yeah!" Marko exclaimed. "Matter of fact, it did. I thought of all the great stuff

I've done already. And here I was, a senior standing before my adult life with a brilliant future. It didn't seem right that it should be taken from me."

"Well," Alonee remarked, "fortunately it all ended well, and here you are, Marko." She smiled so warmly you'd have thought she really liked Marko.

Jaris couldn't get over Alonee's warm heart. He looked at Sereeta, and she was just shaking her head at Marko's swagger.

As Jaris drove Chelsea home that day, she made an announcement. "The science class is going on a field trip Monday. We'll be back at school at the regular time. We're going in vans. Shadrach is coming too. He's gonna show us some of the natural wonders at this creek. We're all excited, but Falisha's mad. She doesn't want to have anything to do with Shadrach. I tell you, Jaris, sometimes people make me sick. Don't they make you sick sometimes?"

"You can say that again," Jaris agreed. "Shadrach is helping Falisha with her algebra. Doesn't that count for anything with the kid?"

"I don't get it, Jaris," Chelsea went on. "Most of us don't even notice Shadrach's scars anymore. I've gotten so used to him that he looks handsome to me. Falisha is such a dummy sometimes. Between her and Inessa, I'd like to scream."

"I think it's because she just doesn't want her mom dating a guy, chili pepper," Jaris suggested. "She's afraid they'll get married and then her life'll be different."

"Yeah," Chelsea replied, "I guess that's it."

"Does Falisha remember her real dad, Chelsea?" Jaris asked.

"No, she doesn't," Chelsea answered. "But she's got his picture and stuff. She's got this fantasy that he's nice and maybe she could go live with him. I guess I understand how she feels. I mean, I'd hate for our family to change."

Chelsea turned and looked at Jaris. "I'm excited about the field trip except old Kanika Brewster is going too. Jare, how come there's always people like that spoiling things."

CHAPTER SIX

The next Monday, Chelsea and Athena Edson, her best friend, rode in Mrs. Colbert's van. Mrs. Colbert was the freshman science teacher. She really liked Shadrach, the scarred war veteran who ran the opossum refuge in town. He also tutored Tubman students in algebra. Chelsea and Athena worked as volunteers at the center, and they loved it.

Chelsea was hoping some of her other friends would join them in the van. Maybe Keisha, Falisha, or Inessa would hop in. But, instead, Kanika Brewster and her catty friend, Hana, piled in. Kanika had been a thorn in Chelsea's side since grade school.

"Move over, fatso," Kanika ordered Chelsea. "Don't hog the whole seat with your fat behind." Chelsea was enraged. She was not fat, but during the summer she gained about three pounds. The extra weight bothered her.

"I'm not fat!" Chelsea snapped. Kanika—in Chelsea's opinion at least— was really ugly, though not everyone agreed. Kanika reminded Chelsea of a big, mean house cat with round, arrogant eyes.

"I don't need a tutor in algebra," Kanika boasted. "I understand everything Mr. Tidwell says in class. You need a tutor, Chelsea 'cause you're dumb. Is your whole family dumb? Usually that runs in families. My parents are very smart. My father is an accountant. He can really do math."

Hana sneered at Chelsea. "Your father's a garage mechanic, right?" she sneered. "My father is an accountant too. He helps people with their money."

"Most accountants are cheats," Athena declared. "That's what I heard. They trick people and steal their money." Athena didn't really believe that. She was just trying to be loyal to Chelsea who was being attacked and was so angry that she was tongue-tied.

"My father is not a cheat," Kanika snarled so loudly that Ms. Colbert heard her.

"No arguing, girls," Ms. Colbert commanded. "Let's talk about something pleasant and not be trying to play one-upmanship on our fathers' jobs. We're going to be visiting a very interesting little creek. Shadrach has graciously agreed to come along and help us understand the ecosystem."

"Ecosystem," Kanika started to say, "that means—"

"I *know* what it means," Chelsea snapped bitterly. "You don't know everything, Kanika. I bet I know a lot of stuff you never heard of!"

They drove up a winding road, then down into a valley with thick trees and shrubs. As everybody got out of the vans,

Chelsea and Athena hurried away from Kanika and Hana. They joined their friends, Keisha and Falisha, and the boys, Heston Crawford and Maurice Moore. Chelsea had a crush on Heston. Chelsea looked around at her friends and said, "It's so good to be with you guys. I was trapped in the van with Kanika and Hana all the way here!"

When the group was assembled, Shadrach led the way down to the bottom of the canyon. Once there, they saw an all-year stream winding its way past them. One group of students went with Shadrach, while the other went with Ms. Colbert. Chelsea was glad to be with Shadrach. Kanika and Hana were with the other group.

"You got a desert environment around here," Shadrach announced. "Not much rain. The animals are cottontail rabbits, lizards, snakes. Some coyotes come down from the hills to water here. Might even get a bobcat."

"What kind of snakes?" Athena asked.

"A lot of rattlesnakes," Shadrach replied. "To tell the truth, that's all I've seen around here. When you're walking, keep on the trail. No going off into the brush and stepping in places where you can't see. You could startle a rattler, and he might strike out of fear. Generally, though, they don't want to meet you anymore than you want to meet them."

Chelsea hadn't seen Kanika leave her group and join Shadrach's group. Suddenly, there she was with her loud mouth. "My mother told me rattlesnakes are very aggressive," she declared. "They hang from the bushes waiting for people to come by. Then they strike. Mom says they can strike from far away."

"Well," Shadrach replied, "that's not true. Rattlesnakes do not hang from bushes waiting for people."

"My mother is very intelligent," Kanika insisted. "She's been to college, and she knows about *everything*. She's *never* wrong. Did *you* go to college, Mr. Shadrach?"

In all the time she had known Shadrach, Chelsea never saw anger in the man's eyes. But she saw it now. "Yes, I've been to college," he replied tersely. "But I've learned a lot more about wildlife firsthand, by dealing with them."

"Well, my mother said a rattlesnake might just run after a person to try to bite them," Kanika persisted.

Shadrach's anger faded into a smile, which he tried to cover. "*Run?*" he asked. Everybody giggled at the mental picture of a rattlesnake running like a dog.

"My father is very well educated too," Kanika continued. "He has a master's degree. Do you have one of those, Mr. Shadrach?"

"No," the man answered dryly. "I had something else to do at the time that seemed more important." Chelsea knew what he was talking about. He was fighting in Iraq.

"My father says nothing is more important than education," Kanika chirped in her strident voice. "I intend to go to college and probably get a Ph.D."

"That's wonderful," Shadrach said.

"Yeah, 'cause I'm very smart. I get all As," Kanika announced. She looked at Shadrach then and asked, "Were you hurt in a fight, Mr. Shadrach? Somebody told me you were in a bad fight. That's how you lost your eye and stuff."

Chelsea wanted to strangle Kanika. Even Athena, who was pretty bold, was shocked at Kanika's insensitive question.

"I guess you could say I was in a fight, yeah," Shadrach answered with a strange look on his face.

"See, I *knew* it," Kanika crowed, turning to Chelsea with a knowing sneer. Chelsea wanted to grab Kanika and hold her head in the creek. But Kanika had more to say to Shadrach. "Were you hurt in those riots in Los Angeles, Mr. Shadrach? I heard that there were a lot of gang fights in Los Angeles, and people got hurt bad."

"No," Shadrach responded, "my fight was in Basra."

"Is that a street in Los Angeles, Mr. Shadrach?" Kanika asked.

"That's a place in Iraq, stupid," Maurice Moore yelled out, unable to take it any longer. "Mr. Shadrach was a soldier in Iraq, fool!"

Shadrach turned to Maurice and said, "We don't use that kind of language, Maurice." But Shadrach didn't seem too upset by Maurice's words. Chelsea and most of the other students were doubled over, laughing at Kanika's ignorance. Kanika looked enraged. Shadrach looked at them. His mouth looked stern, but his one eye was filled with laughter too. "Back to business, gang," he ordered. "We don't want to waste anymore time here, or some snake might come running along."

Shadrach walked on, his group behind him. Kanika had hurried away to rejoin the other group. Chelsea looked for rattlesnakes running after her, but she didn't see any.

"If we're lucky and we look up, we might see a red-tailed hawk circling," Shadrach advised. "These birds find a rising air current, and they circle in that current while they look for prey. They're looking for anything that moves down here. They'll take mammals, snakes, birds, and, if they're hungry enough, even large insects."

Chelsea spotted a red-tailed hawk minutes later. "I see one circling up there," she pointed.

"Make a note of that in your journal," Shadrach told her.

Chelsea leaned over to Athena and whispered, "You think it might get Kanika?"

Athena giggled wildly.

At the end of the field trip, Ms. Colbert gathered both groups in a park near the entrance to the wildlife area. She lectured about the flora and fauna in the area. All the while, Chelsea could feel Kanika's mean cat eyes glaring at her.

When the vans returned to Tubman High, Chelsea jumped out. She could see Jaris already there waiting for her, leaning on his Honda. She saw something else too. Vanessa Allen was walking toward Jaris.

"Jaris, you got a minute?" Vanessa asked.

"Sure," Jaris replied. Just looking at the girl turned him off. He was suspicious of her. He figured she was bad news for Trevor. He knew she would continue to be until Trevor had the sense to cut her loose.

Vanessa wasn't smiling. "Jaris," she scolded, "I don't know how you managed to do it. But you messed up my date with Trevor on Friday night. We had all kinds of great plans, and he called me at the last minute. He seemed really upset. He was sounding real weird and saying he was sick. But you did it. You came to the coffee shop and almost threatened me. Then somehow you managed to mess up Friday for me."

"Why don't you ask Trevor what happened?" Jaris responded calmly. "He'd know more about it than I do."

"Jaris, don't be cute, okay?" Vanessa advised. "I know you don't like me, and that's okay. You got a right to your opinion. But it's not fair to get between Trevor and me. I mean, you've got no right."

"I don't know what you're talkin' about, girl," Jaris responded, spotting Chelsea on her way over. He yelled at her, "Come on chili pepper, let's go."

"Jaris, you're not gonna get away with this," Vanessa declared. "Trevor and me, we got a good thing going. Y'hear what I'm saying? He's the best guy I ever knew, and you're not going to spoil it." Her features had a hard coldness, as if they'd been chiseled out of a block of ice.

Jaris snapped at her, "Have a nice day." Then he turned to his sister and opened the door of the Honda. "Have a good field trip, chili pepper?"

"Yeah," Chelsea answered. "We went down to the creek with Shadrach and Ms. Colbert, and we saw a lot of cool stuff." Chelsea glanced nervously at Vanessa, who continued to stand there looking very angry.

"You're not gonna win this fight, Jaris Spain," Vanessa insisted. "You might be Trevor's friend, but I'm his chick. It's chick over guy pal every time. Trust me!" She turned then and marched off, getting into an old convertible. As she screeched away, she took a lot of rubber off her tires.

"What's she so mad about?" Chelsea asked.

"Oh, she's dating Trevor Jenkins and she's not good for him," Jaris explained, getting behind the wheel.

"How come, Jare?" Chelsea asked.

"She's a gimmie-girl, chili pepper," Jaris replied. "Kinda chick who dates a guy 'cause he'll buy her stuff she can't afford to buy for herself. She's greedy, and she wants money and stuff from Trevor. That's not cool."

"Yeah," Chelsea said. "Trevor's mom works so hard. Me and Mom saw her in the market the other day. She was so tired she was like leaning onto the shopping cart for support. Remember when me and Athena and Inessa sang at the nursing home where Mrs. Jenkins works? All the poor nurses were running around like crazy trying to do for all the patients. Trevor isn't rich. Why doesn't Vanessa buy her own stuff?"

"She should, but she's a leech," Jaris snarled. "You know what a leech is, don't you, chili pepper?"

"Yeah," Chelsea chirped, "these bugs that latch onto people and suck their blood. Shadrach told us there were leeches in the little creek we saw today. Some people go swimming, and all of a sudden there are leeches on them. It's yucky."

"Yeah," Jaris affirmed, "that's what Vanessa is. Trevor is my buddy, and I don't want no leeches sucking on him."

"I like Trevor too," Chelsea remarked. "He's always been nice to me. I like all the Jenkins boys. The other day when he was home, Desmond—Trev's brother—came to school and talked about Afghanistan."

"But," Jaris said to himself, "Trevor isn't like the other Jenkins boys. Ordinarily, Trevor Jenkins had good sense," Jaris thought. Meeting Vanessa had changed all that. He couldn't think clearly anymore. Jaris didn't respond to Chelsea's comments.

The next day in English class, Langston Myers had a sour expression on his face. He had corrected all the English tests, and they were a great disappointment to him. "A few of you did well on the test, but many of you did a terrible job," Mr. Myers fumed. "Some of you did so poorly I'd like to send you back to freshman English. It's hard to believe you're seniors."

Mr. Myers proceeded down the aisles, handing back the tests. He slapped down Jaris's test. He got an A minus. Jaris then happened to glance at Trevor's paper. He was shocked to see a big red F. In all the time Jaris had known Trevor, he never got less than a C in anything. Trevor was a good student, and he usually made Bs.

"Man," Trevor remarked after class, "that dude is a hard grader. He makes old Pippin seem like a good guy."

"What'd you screw up on, Trev?" Jaris asked.

"I don't know," Trevor said. "I thought I did okay."

Jaris glanced at Trevor's paper. "Dude, you left the essay question answer blank. You didn't write anything, and that was worth forty percent of the test."

"Yeah," Trevor admitted sadly. "He wanted examples of poets from the Harlem Renaissance. I kept thinking of that other renaissance, you know, in Europe after the middle ages. I just drew a blank. So I didn't write anything."

"Myers lectured a coupla times about the Harlem Renaissance. Remember?"

Jaris said. "The stuff about Langston Hughes and Claude McKay and those guys?"

"Yeah, that's right," Trevor recalled, grimacing. "What was I thinking about? I feel like such an idiot."

Jaris knew what Trevor was thinking about, but he didn't say anything. Trevor was thinking about just one thing twenty-four-seven. His mind was on Vanessa Allen and what he could do to please her. Jaris figured Trevor was not getting enough sleep or enough time to study. He knew that Trevor had asked Neal at the Chicken Shack to give him shifts six days a week, instead of the four days he usually worked. Neal had frowned and asked, "Is that a good idea, kid?"

"I need the money," Trevor explained.

Jaris knew Neal, the manager of the Chicken Shack. Neal was in his late thirties. He took a personal interest in his workers, most of them teenagers. He took pride in their later success. "Trevor, you're a good worker," he'd said. "But you got a future outside this chicken joint. You need to do well in school and graduate. Senior year's tough. I'm not giving you so many hours that you flunk school, dude."

The next day, the posse gathered at lunch, and Trevor was unusually quiet. He ate his lunch and then took off. He said he needed to do more studying at the library, but Jaris wasn't so sure about that. Jaris begged off staying with his friends too. He trailed Trevor as he climbed the path from the eucalyptus trees.

Trevor wasn't headed for the library. He was going toward the Tubman school parking lot. Jaris stayed out of sight as Trevor hurried to Vanessa's convertible. She'd been waiting for him.

They quickly embraced. Trevor hugged and kissed her as if he couldn't let her go. Jaris couldn't hear what they were saying, but Vanessa was clinging to Trevor and talking excitedly. Trevor seemed to be frustrated. He kept shaking his head. Vanessa seemed to be pleading with him. Jaris figured Vanessa was putting on the pressure to get that necklace. And Trevor was feeling the pressure.

Finally, Trevor got out of the car. Vanessa drove off while Trevor returned to the Tubman campus for his afternoon classes. He walked hunched over, as if he bore the weight of the world on his shoulders. She'd probably made him feel bad for letting her down, Jaris figured.

Jaris headed for his own afternoon classes. "Oh man," Jaris thought, "if Vanessa messes up Trevor's mind so bad that he flunks all his classes, he wouldn't get to graduate. He'll have to come back and do summer school to earn enough credits. All his plans for the community college will be on hold."

Jaris wanted to help Trevor, but he didn't know how. Talking to him only made matters worse. So Jaris waited until classes were over for the day. He dropped Chelsea home and once again drove to the coffee shop where Vanessa worked. He was hoping that maybe she really cared for Trevor just a tiny bit. Maybe she wasn't pure greed. He was hoping he could reach her in some way.

When Vanessa saw Jaris coming into the shop, her expression turned hostile. He ordered an iced coffee and sat at the counter as he'd done before. As usual, the place was almost empty. Nobody in the neighborhood could afford gourmet coffee.

"Look Vanessa, I didn't come to argue, okay?" Jaris began. "I'm just worried about Trevor. You say you care about him, and I'm counting on that. Maybe we can work together to help the guy. He's flunking English, and I'm thinking he might not even graduate Tubman at this rate."

Vanessa shrugged. "So what? High school is just a waste of time anyway. I dropped out when I was in tenth grade and I'm doing fine."

"Vanessa," Jaris explained, "kids without high school diplomas go from one chump-change job to another. These days, a high school diploma isn't enough. You need some college. But heaven help the poor fools without even a high school diploma. Don't you want what's best for your boyfriend, babe?"

"A lot of kids drop out," Vanessa insisted. "I've told Trevor he's stupid to be wasting time in high school. He could work full-time right now and make lots of money. What's he learning at Tubman? Stupid poems in English and old stories about guys who lived a hundred years ago in history. It's all a crock. He'd be smart to just ditch it now and work."

"You're really out to derail the guy, aren't you, Vanessa?" Jaris asked sadly. "You're a guy's worst nightmare. Trevor had plans. He wanted to go to the community college like his brother, Tommy. What are you telling him to do? Make a life career out of frying chicken wings and selling them?"

"You're some kind of a nerd, Jaris," Vanessa sneered. "Trevor told me how hard you work in those classes at Tubman. Trevor said you make good grades, and you're even in the AP American History class to get college credit. Maybe sticking in high school and going to college will do you some good, but Trevor isn't like you, man. Trevor's a dumb guy. No matter how much he studies and even with a diploma, he's still gonna be a dumb dude."

"He's not stupid, Vanessa," Jaris asserted. "You're all wrong about that. All the time I've known Trevor, he made decent grades. He could go to the community college and learn a trade, like auto mechanic or plumbing or electrical work . . . maybe something with computers. He could have a bright future and have a decent life. You want to take that all away from him, Vanessa? You want to break him down before he's had a chance?"

Vanessa shrugged. "You need to mind your own business, Jaris," she responded. "You're not Trevor's father or even his brother. You got no dog in this race, man. Just get out of the way, and let Trevor and me figure out things. It's a losing battle for you anyway. Trevor is gonna do what I want. It's no contest. I got some plans for him, and he'll go along with them. You can't win, Jaris."

Jaris drank the last of his iced coffee in one big gulp. He got up and left the place. If he had the slightest hope that this girl had any real love for Trevor, that hope was now dashed. She saw Trevor as a stupid fool to be manipulated. She couldn't care less about Trevor's future. When she'd stopped using him, she'd toss him aside like a dirty napkin.

Jaris walked from the shop with his hands swinging at his sides, his fingers forming fists. What she said was the sad truth. No matter how much Jaris cared for his friend, he couldn't win.

CHAPTER SEVEN

When Chelsea saw Falisha in the morning, Falisha looked terrible. She had been crying. Her clothing looked as if she had thrown everything on in a hurry. Her usually nice hair was going off in every direction. She had the worst bed hair Chelsea had ever seen.

"Falisha," Chelsea cried, running to the girl. "What's the matter?"

"Ohhh!" Falisha wailed. "Mom talked to me last night, and she said she loves him!"

Chelsea didn't have to ask who "him" was. It had to be Shadrach. Ms. Colbert, Falisha's mom, and Shadrach had been good friends for a long time. When they were on the opossum night rescue mission,

Chelsea saw Ms. Colbert kissing Shadrach. There was no doubt where it was all going.

"Oh, Chelsea," Falisha cried, "I can't stand it! I don't want my mom to marry Shadrach!"

Chelsea liked Shadrach, and she liked Ms. Colbert too. They were both nice, lonely people who had been through a lot of hard times. Ms. Colbert had been married to a man who abused her, and she had to get away. Shadrach had been engaged to a girl who couldn't go through with the marriage when he got injured so badly in Iraq. Both of them had suffered losses. Chelsea thought it would be a beautiful idea for two such kind, good people to get married. But she couldn't say that to Falisha. She would just be pouring gasoline on flames.

"I'm sorry, Falisha," Chelsea consoled. She so wanted to tell Falisha to give Shadrach a chance. Chelsea knew Falisha would grow to like him as most of the kids at Tubman did. He had scars and was missing an eye, but that was no reason not to like him. Chelsea had said all these things before, and they made no difference to Falisha.

"Did your mom say she was gonna marry Shadrach?" Chelsea asked.

"No, but I know she wants to," Falisha replied. "She was kinda feeling me out, seeing how much I was against it. That's why she didn't come right out and say she was gonna marry him. But I could tell she wants to. Oh Chelsea, I don't know what to do. I don't want to live in our house if she marries him!"

You know, Falisha," Chelsea advised carefully, "the kids who work with Shadrach on the opossum rescue program really love him. And the kids in the class he tutors, you can see how they laugh with him and stuff. Don't you think—"

"No!" Falisha cried. "I won't live in our house anymore if Mom marries him."

A strange look came to Falisha's face. "You know, my real father sometimes sends money and cards and stuff. He doesn't always do it, but last Christmas he sent me a little locket. I know he sorta cares about me. I think I'll write him a letter. I'll ask him if it'd be okay if I went up there and lived with him."

"Falisha!" Chelsea chided. "He was mean to your mom. She had a hard time with him."

"He's probably changed a lot since then," Falisha reasoned. "Maybe he's nice now. They got programs to help people get over being abusive. He's probably a whole different person now, Chelsea. I got some pictures of him. He's real nice looking." Falisha dug in her purse and brought out a snapshot of a thin, smiling man. "Doesn't he look nice, Chelsea?"

"Well, yeah," Chelsea admitted. "But he never told you he wanted you to come live with him, did he?"

"No, but that's Mom's fault," Falisha insisted. "She let him know he wasn't supposed to be in my life anymore and stuff like that. So he stayed away. But Mom sends him letters and pictures of me and tells him how I'm doing in school. So it's not like he doesn't even know me. I know he'd like me, Chelsea." Falisha was speaking in a forlorn voice. "He's my father, and I bet I'd like him too."

"You know, Falisha," Chelsea advised, "the way somebody looks doesn't mean as much as what's in their hearts."

Falisha's face hardened. "I'm not gonna live in that house with Mom and *him*. I'm just not."

Chelsea went to her first class feeling sad. Falisha had no good reason to feel as she did about Shadrach. He was such a good person. But maybe Falisha couldn't help her feelings. Chelsea felt sorry for Falisha and for her mother and for Shadrach. They were all good people. Ms. Colbert and Shadrach seemed sort of made for each other. They were kind and compassionate, and they loved animals and the outdoors. It was sad all around.

Ms. Colbert didn't seem her usual cheerful self in class. She seemed preoccupied.

She didn't smile much. She livened up the class when she laughed and told stories and jokes about science. But today she was all business.

When Chelsea got home from school, she confided in her parents. "I like Ms. Colbert and I like Shadrach. It'd be so cool if they could get together. But I'm so sad that Falisha is all upset about it."

"Has Falisha ever tried to become friends with Shadrach?" Mom asked.

Chelsea replied, "She goes to him for math tutoring like me, but even when he's talking to her, she hardly looks at him."

"Got to be more to it than how the guy looks," Pop interjected. "Yeah, when you first see him, you think, 'Hey, what's with this dude?' But pretty soon it wears off, and he's just another dude. He's such a nice guy. He brought his truck into the garage for a new battery and an oil change. We got to talking. He's an interesting guy. Darnell took to him right away. Pretty soon they were jabbering away about different kinds

127

of engines and fuel efficiency, that kinda stuff. I think the little girl has other kinds of problems."

Mom nodded. "I think you're right, Lorenzo. She's an insecure little girl, and she just doesn't want things to change in her house. In a way, she thinks she'll be losing her mom to a stranger."

"But that's not right, you know," Pop asserted. "This Ms. Colbert, she's had a rough time. A husband who beat up on her, raising a kid by herself. She's got a right to her life now. It'd be different if Shadrach was a creep, but he's a good guy."

"I'd like to help Falisha," Chelsea remarked, "but I don't know what to do or say."

Jaris stood in the doorway and remembered a conversation he once had long ago with Sereeta. Her parents had just divorced. Sereeta was about Falisha's age at the time, and she was messed up over the divorce. The minute her mom brought Perry Manley around, Sereeta disliked him. Sereeta believed that Manley resented her right away too.

Sereeta wanted her mother's exclusive love. Perry Manley wanted Olivia Prince's love too, and he resented the pesky little teenager who was in his way. At the time, Sereeta told Jaris that she hated Perry Manley. If her mother married him, she said, she would run away from home and go live in the mountains.

But just a few days ago, Jaris and Sereeta talked about the situation again. "You know," she reflected, "I think if I hadn't hated Perry so much from the gitgo, it might have been better. I just didn't want a stepfather. It wasn't so much that he was bad or anything. I just didn't want a stranger to come live with Mom and me. It was bad enough that Dad was gone, but now some new guy was fixing to move in. I've been wondering. What if I hadn't been so angry? What if I'd tried a little to like him? Could it all have been different?"

Jaris stepped over toward his little sister. "Chelsea," he suggested, "I think it would be good if Falisha talked to Sereeta. When I pick you up at school tomorrow, Sereeta'll come along. Then we'll ask Falisha if she'd like to join us for a frozen yogurt at the Ice House. Sereeta understands where Falisha is at right now, and she could help."

"Oh Jaris, that'd be great!" Chelsea exclaimed.

The next day was a bad one for Jaris. He learned that Trevor had quit the track team that he loved so much. Coach Curry pleaded with him to stay on because Trevor was such a good runner and getting stronger all the time. But Trevor wouldn't listen. He said he didn't have time for track. He was looking for another part-time job to raise money.

After classes, Sereeta and Jaris walked to his car. Jaris told her about Trevor quitting track.

"That's awful," Sereeta responded. "It brought him so much joy. Doesn't that girl realize she's hurting him?"

"She doesn't care, Sereeta," Jaris stated bitterly.

As they approached Jaris's car, Chelsea came along with Falisha. Chelsea didn't tell Falisha that Sereeta wanted to talk to her. Chelsea was hoping the subject of stepfathers could come up in a natural, unforced way at the Ice House.

At the Ice House, they sat with their strawberry and peach frozen yogurts. Sereeta mentioned, "I saw my stepfather the other day. We talked about how Mom is doing at the rehab place. Mom's doing better every day. We were both happy about that."

Falisha looked up with interest. "You got a stepfather?" she asked.

"Yeah, I got him when I was thirteen," Sereeta replied.

"Mom's trying to stick me with a stepfather," Falisha said. "It makes me so sick I can't stand to think about it."

"I hear you," Sereeta responded. "I hated my stepfather so much, I'm telling you. There wasn't a kid in the world who hated having a stepfather more than me. I mean, I didn't even try to make friends with him. Well, pretty soon he hated me too. We had a mutual hate society going."

Falisha was quiet for a moment, staring at her peach yogurt. Then she spoke. "This guy who wants to be my stepfather has tried to be friendly with me. But I don't want anything to do with him, Sereeta. Why didn't you go live with your real dad when the stepfather came?"

Sereeta shrugged. "My father got remarried too. He wasn't too crazy about a teenager coming to live with his new wife and their kids."

"Maybe I'll go live with my real father if Mom marries this guy I hate," Falisha told Sereeta. "I mean, I don't really hate him, but . . ."

"I bet your mom would feel bad if you moved away," Sereeta suggested. "She'd miss you."

"No," Falisha protested with deep anger, "she just cares about that old Shadrach."

Sereeta took a spoonful of strawberry yogurt and then said, "When my mom married this guy, I stayed mad at him. I thought Mom didn't care about me anymore, or she wouldn't have married Perry. I got real nasty, and they were mad. Then I got angrier. It just got worse and worse. Pretty soon they wanted to be rid of me, Falisha."

Sereeta took a small spoonful of her yogurt. "My mom," she went on, "is sick now in the hospital, and she's getting better. So she'll be home pretty soon. Anyway, my stepfather called me up the other night. He asked me if I wanted to have coffee with him and talk. I said no at first, but then he said he really needed to talk to me. So I went."

Jaris cocked his head toward at Sereeta. She hadn't told him about the meeting with Perry Manley. He was hearing about it now for the first time. He listened with interest.

"Anyway, Falisha," Sereeta went on, "here I was going to coffee with the stepfather I hated. I've disliked him for more than four years. I was really nervous. I only did it 'cause I thought it might help Mom when she got home. And, you know what? For the first time in all these years, I saw Perry Manley as a real human being. He was more nervous than I was. He's scared 'cause he knows I've never liked him, that I didn't want him in our life from the beginning."

Falisha could not take her eyes off Sereeta. She listened intently.

"I still don't really like him much," Sereeta went on. "I mean, we'll probably never be buddies. But I don't hate him anymore. We were talking about making things better for Mom when she got home. I promised I'd come for dinner sometimes, and it'd be okay if he was there. I'd still want to go on trips with Mom—just her and me—but maybe eventually we could all go on a trip—you know, *together*. It could be Mom and my stepfather, me, and their baby Jake."

Sereeta stopped, and she almost cried. But then she continued. "You know what makes me feel worse than anything, Falisha? I'm thinking if we'd talked like that years ago . . . if we'd tried—just tried to be nice to each other—maybe I wouldn't have hurt so much thinking nobody cared about me. Maybe Mom wouldn't have cracked up so bad."

Falisha didn't say anything. The conversation turned to small talk, and they all finished their yogurts.

Jaris drove them all home. Just before being dropped off at her house, Falisha leaned over and whispered to Chelsea. "I never want to be friends with Shadrach. *Never!* I'm gonna write a letter to my father and ask him if I can come live at his house if Mom marries Shadrach." Then Falisha got out of the car, slammed the door, and ran to her house.

Everyone in the car slumped back in their seats, defeated. Sereeta and Jaris had both heard what Falisha had whispered to Chelsea. Jaris felt bad that Sereeta had tried so hard and apparently failed to convince Falisha.

"You did your best, Sereeta," Jaris said. "Thanks."

But Sereeta smiled and said, "She's normal. I wouldn't have been so easily convinced when I was her age. But she's gonna think about what I said, maybe tonight or tomorrow night."

Jaris pulled the car away from the curb and started driving Sereeta home. They drove in silence for a few minutes. Then Jaris started talking about what was on his mind.

"Sereeta," Jaris remarked, "I'm getting really worried about Trevor. I found out today that he quit the track team. And he hardly talks to his old friends anymore. He's always rushing to meet that witch."

"That's such a shame," Sereeta responded. "Seeing Trevor run in those meets, it was so much fun. Him and Kevin and Matson were such a wonderful group. Coach Curry was counting on Trevor being a big part of Tubman victories. Nobody even knows yet if Marko can run in the meets yet."

"I see Vanessa hanging in the parking lot way before school gets out," Chelsea chimed in. "I can see the parking lot from science."

Jaris and Sereeta exchanged knowing glances.

"What can we do, babe?" Jaris asked. "It breaks my heart to think how hard Trevor has worked for good grades and how he dreamed of college and a future. Now she's draining it all out of him. He's right at the finish line when all the good stuff is about to happen for him. She's just made him stumble bad."

"The other day I heard Kevin Walker yelling at him," Sereeta added. "Kevin was telling Trevor to wake up and lose that 'parasite chick.' But it didn't help. The two guys almost came to blows."

"I don't know what it'll take for Trevor to wake up," Jaris remarked sadly. "I hope by the time he does wake up it's not too late."

That night, when Jaris went to work at the Chicken Shack, Trevor was already there. There were quite a few customers, and everybody was hustling.

Jaris noticed that Trevor wasn't as efficient as usual. He mixed up an order, giving someone chicken wings instead of nuggets. The guy cursed Trevor. Usually Trevor would have had the cool to be professional. He'd just blow it off. But now he looked mad, and he gave the guy as good as he got.

Luckily, Neal didn't see the exchange, or Trevor would have been in serious trouble. Neal wouldn't stand for any of his employees being rude even if with unreasonable customers.

A little bit later, it happened again. A woman was trying to decide whether she wanted creamy ranch dressing or vinaigrette on her salad. She kept going back and forth until Jaris heard Trevor snarl, "Make up your mind lady."

This time Neal saw it too. He said to Trevor, "See me after your shift is done, Trevor."

Trevor looked at Jaris, misery on his face, "Oh man, now I'm in for it," he moaned.

Later in the evening Trevor gave a couple crispy instead of grilled chicken, and they complained loudly. Trevor had never got so many orders mixed up. He was acting like a zombie. Jaris figured he was on so many late dates with Vanessa, and she was always pressuring him for something. Trevor was just not getting enough sleep. His brain was fried.

Trey, a shift supervisor, came up alongside Jaris. "What's with that guy?" he asked. "Is he on drugs or something? He's your friend, Spain. What's going on?"

"No, no, he's just tired," Jaris answered quickly. "We had a lot of homework, and the senior year is just underway. He hasn't organized his time yet. He'll be okay."

"Well, he better get his act together pretty quick," Trey declared. "Neal's pretty upset. He's tired of the dude making mistakes and losing us customers. Too many good kids out there looking for work to put up with somebody like him."

"Trevor's always been really good here," Jaris countered.

"Yeah, well that was then. This is now," Trey snapped. "He was good before. Now, not so good."

Both Jaris and Trevor got off work at the same time. Jaris hung around outside for a few minutes, waiting for Trevor to finish having his talk with Neal. Jaris figured Trevor would need some support.

When Trevor finally came out, he looked grim. "They're cuttin' my hours, man," he told Jaris. "I wanted more hours so I got more money in my paycheck. Now they're cuttin' me. Neal said I'm makin' too many mistakes. And then I yelled at that woman who wanted a different salad dressing every minute. Neal said I need to shape up, or I'm through here. Man, I don't know what I'd do without this job." Trevor was breathing hard and shaking.

"Take it easy, Trevor. Everybody has a bad night once in a while," Jaris consoled him. "You'll be okay, man."

Jaris glanced into the parking lot. Usually Trevor came in his brother's car, but Jaris didn't see it.

"I'll give you a lift home, Trev. I don't see your car there," Jaris suggested.

"Vanessa dropped me off," Trevor replied. "She's gonna pick me up."

His eyes were filled with worry. "The poor kid. She's got troubles too. Those freakin' jerks at the coffee shop fired her too. Said she wasn't learning fast enough. She splits her rent with another girl, and it's coming due in two days. I was gonna help her with that."

"Dude," Jaris spoke softly, "I'm worried about you. I'm worried sick, man. If something happened to you, I'd have trouble holdin' on, y'hear what I'm sayin', dude?"

CHAPTER EIGHT

Vanessa's car sped into the parking lot. Trevor broke from Jaris and went running toward her. As Jaris got into his Honda, he saw Vanessa jump from her car and march toward Trevor. They spoke for a minute. Then Jaris heard Vanessa yelling.

"You don't got the money, Trevor? You said you were gonna get more hours, and your boss was gonna give you an advance. Did ya get it? Brandee's on my case for the rent, Trevor. She says if I don't come up with the money she's gonna throw all my stuff in the street!"

Jaris was frozen halfway into the car. He couldn't stop watching Vanessa play out her scene.

"Babe, I tried to get more hours," Trevor whined. "But Neal was ticked off 'cause I made a few mistakes tonight with the customers. He wouldn't give me no advance. I tried, babe, I swear it. I get paid on Monday, and I'll have the money for you then."

Vanessa started beating on Trevor's chest with her fists, "Listen to me!" she screamed. "I need the money now! Don't you understand me? *I need it now!*"

Trevor was distraught. "Babe I—" he stammered.

"You promised me, Trevor!" she wailed. "You said you'd have the cash tonight. Brandee's gonna throw my stuff out. She's mean enough to do it. Am I supposed to live in my car or go to some freakin' shelter?"

Jaris felt like walking over and telling Vanessa Allen what he thought of her. But he knew doing that would just humiliate Trevor all over again. Jaris figured his friendship with Trevor was already on very thin ice.

"Maybe I can get some money for you, babe," Trevor whined. "Give me a coupla hours."

"You know what, Trevor?" Vanessa cried. "I love you so much. I really love you, man. But if you can't be there for me, I gotta find someone who will."

Trevor took a step back from Vanessa, not believing what he was hearing. Vanessa just went on.

"There's a dude used to come in the Ice House when I worked there," she bellowed at him. "He was crazy about me. He still calls me all the time. He dropped outta high school a long time ago, and now he's makin' real money. I ask him for help, he'll have the money for me in a minute. If you can't be there for me when I'm in trouble, Trevor, then maybe I should just call this other dude. I don't love him like I love you, but a girl has to look out for herself. Y'hear what I'm sayin'?"

"No, Vanessa," Trevor pleaded. "Hang in there. Just give me a little more time. I'll

get some money for you. I swear I will."
Trevor got into the car with Vanessa then,
and they drove off.

Jaris was shaking with rage as he got
into his Honda and drove home. After a
couple of minutes of driving, Jaris decided on what to do. Saturday morning, he
would go see Vanessa's parents. Jaris had
never been to the Allen house, but he
knew where her parents lived. One time,
Trevor told him she lived in a blue house
with daisies in the front yard. Jaris didn't
think he'd have a problem finding such a
house on Mohican Street. Going there was
a stab in the dark, but he didn't have any
other ideas. Maybe the Allen family could
help their daughter—if they hadn't long
since washed their hands of her. Surely
though they'd care if she was on the edge
of homelessness. They'd have to listen if
all that stood between her and the streets
was a poor fool like Trevor Jenkins who
was running himself into a brick wall for
her.

Right after breakfast on Saturday morning, Jaris drove down Mohican Street and found the blue stucco house. A nice, well kept lawn was in the front, and daisies grew along the walkway leading to the front door. Jaris rang the bell and waited. In seconds, a woman came to the door. She smiled pleasantly and said hello.

"Hi," Jaris said, "my name is Jaris Spain, and I'm a senior at Tubman High School."

The woman's smile deepened. "I bet you're selling magazine subscriptions for some trip, right?" she asked.

"No, ma'am," Jaris responded. "I want to talk to you about your daughter, Vanessa."

The woman was not smiling anymore. "She's hasn't lived here for a long time. She's gone to live with her sister somewhere. I don't even know where either of them are."

"Vanessa doesn't live with her sister anymore," Jaris explained. "She's got a roommate, and she's going from job to job. She's gonna be thrown out of her apartment 'cause she has no rent money. She's hangin' with a friend of mine, some poor guy who's still in high school. And she's manipulating him to give her money. She's trying to take this poor guy, sucking the blood out of him. I was just wondering if there was any way you could talk to her or something. Maybe get her back home for a while."

The woman's expression turned cold. "It's none of my business what's going on in my daughter's life now," she declared. "She doesn't have anything to do with us. We did our best, but both our daughters disappointed us bitterly. I'm sorry about your friend, but there's nothing we can do. Vanessa and Dena are the kind of girls who hurt people wherever they go."

Suddenly—unexpectedly —the woman began to cry. "We tried so very hard, my husband and I . . ."

"If Vanessa were out on the street with nowhere to go," Jaris urged, "would you take her in? I mean, she *is* your kid."

"No!" the woman stated flatly. "We would not. She's given us enough grief. The last time she was in this house, she demanded her father give her enough money to go to Las Vegas. When he wouldn't, she screamed at him and upset him so much that . . . the next day he had a massive stroke . . . from which he has never recovered." The woman swung the door wider. Jaris could see a man in a wheelchair, a quilt over his legs. He didn't even look up.

"I'm sorry," Jaris said softly. The woman said nothing. She just closed the door.

Falisha Colbert sat in her bedroom, composing a letter to her father. The last she had heard from him, he was living in Los Angeles, selling real estate. He sent Falisha a photograph of his condo. It looked nice. Falisha felt sure there would be room for her there. She wrote:

Dear Daddy,

Mom is dating a guy I really don't like. His name is Shadrach. If she marries him, I don't want to live here anymore. Could I come live with you? I wouldn't be any trouble. I told Mom how I felt about this guy, but I think she loves him. I don't think Mom loves me as much as she loves this Shadrach guy. Let me know real soon if it would be okay for me to come there and live with you."

Love, Falisha

Falisha's mother looked in the bedroom as Falisha was finishing the letter. "Doing homework, sweetie?" she asked.

"Yeah," Falisha lied, sliding the letter into her math workbook. Mom came into the room and sat down in the rocker that was over to the side. "Sweetie, you feel really bad about me being friends with Shadrach, don't you?" she asked.

Falisha didn't look at her mother. She looked down a the carpet on the floor. "Yeah," she murmured.

"I knew you didn't like him, Falisha," Mom granted. "But I thought, when you got to know him better, you might like him more. Do you know who I love more than anybody else in the whole wide world?"

Falisha shook her head, still staring at the bedspread.

"You, Falisha," Mom assured her. "You're the center of my universe, and you always will be. I would do anything rather than hurt you, baby."

Falisha felt numb. She didn't turn her head. She felt a lump in her throat. She expected her mom to say that she had to marry Shadrach. Then Falisha would have a nice daddy like all children should have. She thought Mom would tell her that she would grow to love Shadrach too because he was such a wonderful man. But Falisha didn't want to hear any of that. All Falisha knew was that, if Shadrach came into the family, he would ruin everything. She didn't want him, and she would never want him.

"Falisha," Mom went on, "I'm going to see Shadrach tomorrow. More kids want to sign up for his opossum rescue shelter. I'm going to stay involved in the opossum program, driving the kids and all. But I'm going to tell Shadrach that we can't be friends anymore like we have been."

Falisha turned her head sharply and stared at her mother. Falisha couldn't believe her own ears. "You're not gonna marry him?" Falisha gasped.

"We're not going to see each other anymore except on a professional level, Falisha," Mom replied. "If you feel that strongly about this, I'm not going to bring unhappiness into your life. You're my precious little girl. You're the most important person in my life. Your happiness means more to me than anything else."

Falisha jumped up from the bed, ran to her mother, and hugged her. Tears streamed down Falisha's face. She kept saying to her mother, over and over, "I love you, Mommy. I love you so much!" Then, when Falisha's mother was gone, Falisha tore up the letter to her father. It was in such small bits that nobody could ever piece it together again.

At school on Monday, Falisha rushed to tell Chelsea what had happened. "Mom broke up with Shadrach," Falisha said breathlessly. "Can you believe it, Chelsea?"

"Wow! What happened?" Chelsea asked. By then, Athena and Keisha had joined them. "Shadrach isn't dating Ms. Colbert anymore," Chelsea told them.

"Mom said she was doing it for me," Falisha explained. "She said she was breaking up with him 'cause it made me so unhappy. Mom said she loves me more than anybody. I didn't think she'd do that for me in a million years. I thought she loved Shadrach more than she loved me."

"Wow!" Chelsea exclaimed again. She wasn't sure what she felt. It was good that

Ms. Colbert loved Falisha so much that she would give up her boyfriend. But it was sad too. Chelsea liked Ms. Colbert and Shadrach, and she wanted them to be happy too.

When Chelsea got home from school, she told her parents what happened.

"Falisha is so happy her mom is breaking up with Shadrach. Her mom's doing it 'cause it's making Falisha unhappy," Chelsea announced.

"Well," Chelsea's mother commented, "Ms. Colbert is giving up her own happiness for the sake of her child's. That's very commendable."

"When Falisha is older, she'll skip off to college," Pop remarked. "Maybe those two—Ms. Colbert and Shadrach—got another crack at it, eh? When Falisha is in college, Ms. Colbert can look up opossum man, and that little girl ain't gonna care. That's what—four years off? That ain't so bad."

"Yeah," Chelsea answered, "but it makes me sad too. Ms. Colbert and

Shadrach seemed so happy together. I saw them kissing. They were so cute."

"Don't be spyin' on people kissing, little girl," Pop scolded. "And don't you be getting any ideas either. Don't you be kissin' up with some of those little punks down there at Tubman. I know how those slick little punks are. They think they're big stuff."

Pop was on a roll. "Even Darnell, down at the garage. He's almost twenty and he's a good kid. Well, little girl, you come down to the garage the other day with Jaris, 'member? You know what Darnell said? His eyeballs popped, and he goes, 'Hey, who's that hot chick there with your son?' 'I go, Hey, hey, hey! Watch yourself, dude. That happens to be my little girl. She's not for lookin' at, especially by twenty-year-old dudes like you.' And Darnell, he gets all nervous, like I'm gonna haul off and punch him or something. And I mighta if he hadn't of backed off with that kinda talk. 'I didn't know she was your daughter, boss,' he's slobberin'. 'I'm *sorry.*'"

A glow came over Chelsea's face. "Did he *really* say I was a hot chick?" she asked.

"Yeah," Pop growled. "The punk is lucky I didn't pour a pail of water over his head to cool him down. Nobody calls my little girl a 'hot chick' no second time. Not if he figures to live long enough to get Social Security."

Chelsea raced to her room and texted Athena, Keisha, and Falisha. She told them that the cute guy at Spain's Auto Care, who is almost twenty, called her a "hot chick." Chelsea had glanced at Darnell a few times when she visited her father's garage. She noticed he was tall and handsome. It made her day that he said such a thing about her, a little fourteen-going-on-fifteen-year-old freshman. Chelsea went to her mirror and looked at herself with new respect. She was really growing up.

"You go, girl!" she giggled.

On her last shopping trip, Jaris had made her buy medium tops instead of small. Now she was almost glad he did. She was already pushing the seams of the medium sizes. It was time to go shopping again.

Jaris got the call later that evening.

"Jaris," Mickey Jenkins said, her voice shaky, "my boy ain't been home at all. I ain't seen him since Friday. He never come home from his work. Tommy out lookin' for him now. You seen Trevor, Jaris?"

Jaris hadn't seen Trevor in school. But he figured Trevor was home sick—or just plain tired.

"Last I seen him was at the Chicken Shack Friday night," Jaris replied. "He . . . uh . . . left about the same time I did. That was around ten thirty, Mrs. Jenkins."

"He never come home, Jaris," Mrs. Jenkins repeated. "He never done that before. No call. No nothin'. I come home from the nursin' home, and I didn't even go to bed. I waited and waited for him to come home. I prayed 'n' cried, boy. But he didn't come home, not Saturday nor Sunday. Jaris, how did he get home from the job, Friday? He didn't borrow Tommy's car like usual." Mrs. Jenkins' voice was heavy with sadness.

Jaris swallowed. "Vanessa Allen. She dropped him off and picked him up. She was gonna take him home."

"He never come, Jaris," Mrs. Jenkins said again. "I'm just sick. I'm afraid somethin' happen to my baby." She was crying now.

"I'll start looking for him, Mrs. Jenkins," Jaris promised. "I'll start right now."

"Thank you, boy. Thank you," Trevor's mother said. "You let me know if you hear anything."

Jaris's parents were in the living room when he came from his bedroom. Jaris had his car keys out.

"Where you off to boy?" Pop asked. "I thought you didn't work tonight."

"Trevor Jenkins is missing," Jaris responded. "His mother just called me. He didn't get home Friday night, and he's been gone all weekend. No phone call to his mom or anything. She's really worried."

Pop frowned. "He's goin' nuts over that no-good skirt. That's his problem, Jaris. They came by the garage the other day. She was readin' him the riot act 'cause he didn't have the cash to fix her beater. Nothin' makes a fool of a man like a chick like her."

Jaris didn't know what to say. Of course, he agreed with Pop.

"Now did that Mickey Jenkins call the police?" Pop asked.

"She didn't say, but I don't think so," Jaris answered. "I think she's afraid to get the cops involved."

Pop shook his head and sighed. "Bad business! Just bad business!" he commented.

"I'm gonna look around some of the places we've hung out," Jaris said.

"Be careful, Jaris," Mom advised. "It's going to be completely dark soon. At night, the bad element comes out." Jaris knew what his mother meant—the gangbangers. Crime went up sharply once the sun went down. Thieves were out too, looking for easy money. The open-all-night places were easy pickings for thieves.

Terrible fears assailed Jaris as he got into his Honda. With the state of mind Trevor was in, Vanessa could talk him into anything. He seemed frantic to get her some money on Friday night. Would Vanessa get Trevor involved in a crime again? It could happen again, only this time Trevor might not be so lucky.

Trevor had had enough brains to dump Vanessa back then. Now he was in deeper. The web Vanessa had woven around him was stickier and tighter now. Trevor seemed helpless. He would do whatever she asked, regardless of what happened. Jaris felt panicky. He had a terrible, sinking feeling that Trevor might have gone beyond the point of no return.

He started up the car and drove over to Pequot Street. No Trevor. He pulled over to the curb to decide what to do next. He took out his cell phone and called Tommy Jenkins.

"Tommy, I'm on Pequot Street, huntin' for Trevor. Your mom called me. I was hoping maybe he's jogging around here. Thought he might be running off some steam, but I don't see anybody."

"I've been on every freakin' street in the neighborhood," Tommy groaned. "Ma's nearly crazy. She's got high blood pressure anyway, and she don't need this, Jaris. Her blood pressure is really up. I'm trying to get her to go to the emergency room, but she won't go. All she wants is to find that idiot brother of mine. Ma's worked so hard all her life. She was just seeing the light—now this. Desmond and Junior and me, we made it. But Trevor had to screw up. Man, if that little creep causes Ma to get sick and die, I'll strangle him with my own hands."

Jaris knew Tommy was just raving. He loved Trevor as much as Ma did. His own fears and frustration were getting the better of him.

"Tommy," Jaris said in a commanding voice, "I'm calling the rest of the guys.

161

We'll all be out looking. Somebody's bound to find something."

"Thanks, man," Tommy responded.

Jaris called Kevin and Oliver and Derrick. They all agreed to join the search. Jaris drove toward the Coffee Camp, a cheap little dive where the boys often grabbed a latte. Maybe Trevor was hanging out there.

CHAPTER NINE

Jaris found a few guys at the Coffee Camp, none of whom he knew. Jaris and his friends came here usually during the late afternoon. Now the crowd was rougher and older. And there was no sign of Trevor.

Jaris got back in his car and made a call.

"Shadrach?" he said.

"Yeah, man. Is this Jaris?" Shadrach asked.

"Yeah," Jaris replied. "Say, listen, my friend Trevor Jenkins has gone missing. Nobody has seen him since late Friday. That's not like him. I last saw him drive off with this bad-news chick, Vanessa Allen, in a beat-up old green convertible. It's got a lot of rear end damage. I don't have a license number."

Shadrach was silent, probably wondering what Jaris wanted. "I was thinking, Shad," Jaris continued, "you might help us find Trevor. If you're out there looking for wounded opossum, keep an eye open for this poor fool. He's a good guy, but he's not thinking too straight now. This is one creepy chick, and she's maybe got him in trouble."

"I hear you, Jaris," Shadrach responded. "Matter of fact, I was just going out on an opossum run. If I see anything I'll get back to you right away."

Shortly after he ended the call, Jaris heard back from Oliver Randall. He'd borrowed his father's car and was cruising around looking for any sign of Trevor. Then Kevin Walker called. He was riding a motorcycle, and he was scouting the neighborhood. Later on, Derrick checked in and said he and Destini were looking too.

Jaris stopped at a ravine where homeless guys hung out. They had little fires going and were heating cans of beans. Jaris knew some of the guys, including a couple of Tubman dropouts. One of them hailed Jaris. It was someone Jaris knew by his nickname, Squint. "Hey, dude," Squint called, "long time, no see. Wassup, man? You still crackin' the books at the factory?"

"Yeah," Jaris answered. "Hey man, I'm huntin' for a friend of mine. He's gone wacko over a bad chick, and he's missin'. You seen a green convertible with rear end damage around here?"

Squint shook his head no. "What's the chick look like?" he asked.

"Hair dyed red," Jaris replied.

"Not too many like that," Squint laughed.

Jaris scribbled his cell phone number on a piece of paper. Then he handed it to Squint with a five dollar bill. "Give me a heads-up if you see anything, bro," he told him.

"Okay!" Squint said, grinning.

Jaris thought about the last time Trevor dated Vanessa, when he was tricked into the drugstore heist. Would Vanessa try to talk him into doing something stupid, like sticking up an all-night deli? Jaris knew Trevor well enough. Trevor wouldn't knowingly do a crime like that. But who knew what lies Vanessa was feeding him?

Then Jaris remembered the bright green stucco building in the picture in Trevor's wallet. It had to be Vanessa's apartment. Jaris decided to take a chance and head there. Maybe her girlfriend hadn't thrown her out yet. Jaris figured Brandee, her roommate, was probably as bad as Vanessa. They might be cooking up something together to raise money. And Trevor would be caught in the middle of it.

After a short drive, Jaris stopped at the apartment. This was the place in the photograph—he was sure of it. He got out of the car, approached the door, and rang the doorbell. Nobody answered. He rapped on the door and got no response. No luck.

Jaris went back to his car and drove to the Ice House. Vanessa used to work there. Maybe she was visiting her old friends, and she and Trevor would be hanging out.

The Ice House was filled with people eating frozen yogurt and smoothies. Jaris approached a waitress. "Excuse me," he said. "Maybe you can help me. I'm looking for some friends of mine. And they coulda come in here. The guy's tall, wears an LA Dodgers baseball cap, backward usually. The chick has dyed red hair."

The girl thought for a minute. Then her face brightened with a recollection. "Yeah!" she replied. "There were people like that in here last night, just before we closed. I noticed her 'cause of that red hair. You see a black chick with flame red hair, and she sorta stands out. They went over to a table and had smoothies."

"Any idea," Jaris probed, "where they might be?"

"They kept talking about going to something on Algonquin Street," the waitress answered. "I guess a party or something. The chick kept saying how rich everybody is on Algonquin Street. She laughed a lot. She coulda been high, I don't know. But the dude with the baseball cap, he looked kinda stunned. He looked like a kid traveling with a faster crowd than he was used to."

"Was it just the guy in the baseball cap and the red-haired chick?" Jaris asked.

"No, there was another couple with them," the girl recalled. "There was another chick and an ugly-looking dude. I was scared of him. He was older than the other three. He was real tall, and he had this straggly beard coming out of his chin, a goatee. He mighta been thirty-something or even older."

The waitress grinned and shook her head. "I was glad when they left. I had this creepy feeling all the time they were here. I even thought maybe they were casing the place or something."

"Thanks a lot!" Jaris said. The ugly dude the girl described sounded like Bo, the boyfriend of Vanessa's sister. The other girl was probably Dena, Vanessa's sister. So they had all hooked up again.

Back in his car, Jaris called all his friends and alerted them. Trevor was probably traveling with Vanessa, her sister Dena, and Dena's sleazy boyfriend, Bo. They were cooking up something that would happen on Algonquin Street. Maybe a burglary. Maybe Vanessa learned of a house over there that had a lot of valuables for the taking. That was possible. She'd been a massage technician at the spa for a short time. She might have found out about some rich people who were going on vacation.

Of course, that's not how Vanessa would put it to Trevor. She would probably tell him that these people were her friends. She'd say that they had invited them all over to spend some time at the house as house-sitters. A lot of people had friends over to house-sit while they were on vacation.

As Jaris drove toward Algonquin Street, he heard his ring tone. It was Alonee. She was riding with Oliver, cruising around in search of Trevor.

"You think they're planning a crime on Algonquin Street, Jaris?" Alonee asked. "I'm sure Trevor wouldn't go along with that."

"Out of love for her, who knows what he'd do?" Jaris commented bitterly. "I'm heading down Algonquin Street now. If I see that busted-up green car parked in front of some house, I might be able to stop Trevor from ruining his life forever."

"Oh, Jaris," Alonee cautioned, "that's dangerous! Don't get in the middle of something where you might get hurt."

"Alonee," Jaris protested, "if Trevor is busted with the others burglarizing a house, it's over for everybody. Everything poor Mickey Jenkins struggled to accomplish is down the drain. I've lost my best friend. And Trevor is serving time. I'm sick just thinking about what might be going down."

Oliver came on the phone then. "We'll meet you over on Algonquin. I think Kevin and Derrick are getting there too. Maybe we'll get lucky and scare them off before they do anything."

As Jaris drove in the darkness toward Algonquin, his thoughts were of Mickey Jenkins and her struggle to raise good boys. So many mothers in the neighborhood had to go to a prison to visit their sons. Mrs. Jenkins swore it would never be that way for her. She told her boys she'd rather have a dead son than one in prison. She raised three fine boys, but now Trevor was on the brink of disaster.

Sirens wailed in the night, and Jaris grew tense. Maybe they were too late. Maybe the crime was underway already. Maybe Alonee's posse would arrive too late to save their friend. Kevin, Oliver, Alonee, Derrick, Destini, and Jaris were all racing down Algonquin Street—hoping against hope they were in time.

But why were the sirens wailing?

An ambulance came screaming down the street. Jaris pulled over to the right to let it go by. Maybe something else had happened, something that had nothing to do with Trevor. An auto accident. Or maybe somebody on Algonquin Street had a heart attack. Jaris didn't see any police cars, just the ambulance. If a crime was in progress, police cars would surely be on the scene.

Jaris heard his ring tone. "Yeah?" he said, grabbing the phone.

"Jaris!" Pop exclaimed. "Your mother is freakin'. You okay? What are you up to out there? What's goin' on, boy? I don't want you puttin' yourself in danger. Trevor's a good kid and all that. But if he's gone nuts over some chick and got himself in hot water, your mom and I don't want you to get scalded. Y'hear what I'm sayin'?"

"I do, Pop. I'm fine!" Jaris assured his father. "We're all out here, Oliver and Kevin and Derrick, even Alonee and Destini. We just think Trevor is hanging somewhere, and he's maybe afraid to go home. He's never stayed out on his ma like this, and he dreads facing her. You know how scared Trevor is of his ma."

Jaris was playing down the seriousness of the situation. He didn't dare tell his father that Trevor was with Vanessa's sister and her crooked boyfriend. He wouldn't dare mention that Trev might be involved a crime.

"Well, you just watch yourself, boy," Pop commanded. "And get home as soon's you can. Your mom is really upset. The later you're out on those mean streets, the more dangerous it gets."

"Yeah, Pop," Jaris responded. "It won't be much longer."

"Keep in touch," Pop demanded.

Jaris glanced at the time. It was almost ten thirty. He was in the middle of Algonquin Street, but he didn't see anything going on. Maybe that waitress got it mixed up. Maybe the conversation was just about how rich the people were over on this street. Could it be that they weren't plotting anything at all?

Oliver's car cruised alongside Jaris's. Alonee looked out the passenger side. "Anything?" she asked.

"Not so far," Jaris reported. "I'm driving over to Arapaho. The houses over there are even nicer. Lotta people on vacation. Some people are so stupid, they go away and don't turn off their paper deliveries. The yards are full of newspapers. It's like telling every thief in town that nobody's home."

Jaris drove down Arapaho Street with Oliver behind him. Then Jaris heard sirens again—this time a lot of them. Jaris felt his legs go numb. Something was going down on the next street, Apache. Jaris turned sharply and made a U-turn. Oliver followed. Before they were at the end of the street, Kevin rode up on his motorcycle. Derrick was right behind him.

The minute they got to Apache Street, they were stopped. There was a lot of police activity at the end of the street. At least four police cruisers were parked in front of a very large house—one of the nicest in the neighborhood. Jaris tried to edge a little closer, but a police officer shouted at him. "Turn around! Nobody past the barricades."

Jaris stopped the car. "What's going on down there, officer?" Jaris asked from the car window.

The officer snapped back, "Nothin' to see, kid. Just turn around and get outta here. We don't need sightseers."

Jaris turned his car around and parked it at the beginning of Apache Street. The others did the same. They all got out of their cars, and Kevin jumped off his bike. They stood in a little knot, staring at the action at the large two-story house at the other end of the street.

"Ohhh!" Alonee gasped with dread in her voice. "I see Vanessa's green car. Do you guys see it? It's in the driveway of that house."

"Oh man, you're right," Jaris groaned. He felt sick to his stomach and light-headed.

"This is bad!" Oliver declared.

Kevin just stood there, a grim look on his face. He liked Trevor. He didn't like many people, but he liked Trevor. They competed against each other on the Tubman track team, but the competition was always friendly. No matter who won, the other would come over with a fist bump or high five.

Several of the people who lived at this end of Apache Street were standing in their front yards and staring at the activity. A middle-aged man commented to one of his neighbors. "Don't the Colliers live in that house where the police are going in?"

"Yes," the neighbor replied, "I guess somebody tried to break in. We heard the alarms going off."

The neighbor's wife added, "The Colliers are on vacation. They own the Sunshine Spa in town."

Jaris overheard the conversation. He made the connection immediately—and his heart sank. Vanessa had briefly worked as a massage therapist at the Sunshine Spa before they let her go. She must have heard about the owners' vacation plans. To her, that meant that the house would be unoccupied.

"The police got here very fast," another man remarked.

"The Colliers have a lot of nice stuff in there," a woman responded. "We've been to parties over there, and they have many beautiful things. Lots of electronics. I bet that's what attracted the thieves."

Then the door of the house opened, and a police officer stepped out on the walk.

"Oliver," Jaris groaned brokenly, "they're bringing people out in handcuffs."

"Yeah," Oliver responded. "Oh brother, this is so bad!"

Jaris didn't want to look. He didn't want to see his lifelong friend being led from the house in handcuffs. He couldn't bear to see Trevor brought so low.

Tears formed in Jaris's eyes. He was shaking. Jaris kept seeing Mickey Jenkins' face when she heard the news. Her worst nightmare was coming true—the one thing she dreaded more than anything else in the world. She had taught Trevor values. She'd taught him right from wrong. How could he have come to this? It seemed so wrong, so unfair.

"I see Vanessa," Alonee pointed. "You can't miss that red hair."

Jaris's heart was pounding. How could Trevor have gone this far? He was a good person. Even out of love for Vanessa, how could he have thrown everything good in his life overboard?

"There's another girl!" Oliver remarked. "Probably the sister. Vanessa's sister."

Jaris expected Trevor and Bo to be next. Jaris was so sick to his stomach, he had to fight off upchucking. He was just so sick in his heart and stomach. His mouth was dry. His lips stuck together.

Jaris heard his ring tone. That'd be Mrs. Jenkins or Tommy, wanting to know whether there was any good news. Jaris didn't think he could tell them the news. How could he say he was standing on Apache Street, waiting to see Trevor led out in handcuffs?

Jaris answered the call.

"Jaris? Shadrach," came the familiar voice.

"Yeah. Hey, Shadrach," Jaris replied barely above a whisper. "Vanessa and the others. They tried to rob a house over here on Apache Street. The cops are leading them out now. Oh man! This's gotta be the saddest day of my life. I think they're gonna be bringing Trevor out next."

"Jaris," Shadrach cut in, "I found him, Trevor. He was in a ravine over here."

Jaris blinked. Found who? What was Shadrach talking about? At this terrible moment, Jaris didn't care about another rescued opossum.

"Jaris, hold on," Shadrach told him. "Here he is."

"Jare?" It was Trevor Jenkins' voice at the other end.

Jaris clamped his right hand over his mouth in shock. The tears in his eyes became a torrent, running down his cheeks.

"Trev?" he gasped. "Where are you, man?" At the sound of Trevor's name, the other kids all turned their heads toward Jaris. He nodded at them and pointed to the phone. He mouthed the words silently, "It's him."

"I'm on Pequot Street, man," Trevor replied. "What's goin' down?"

"Vanessa and Dena and Bo, they tried to rob a house on Apache. The cops are here, bringing them out in cuffs," Jaris answered. "Trevor, I'm freakin'! I thought you were with them! My stomach hurts so bad I'm doubled up!"

"Me helpin' them rob a house?" Trevor asked. "Not me. No way, man. They told me what they wanted to do. Vanessa, she said the guy she used to work for at the spa was on vacation. He had tons of swag, and we could take it and get rich. When I said I wouldn't, I got in a fight with Bo. He don't fight fair. He worked me over pretty good, but I got away. I been hidin' out in the ravine over here. I didn't know what to do. I could not go home to Ma after being missing— and all beat up . . . Shadrach found me."

"You okay?" Jaris asked.

"Yeah," Trevor replied. "I'm banged up pretty good. I got a black eye and some bruises. My lip is cut and swelled up. I thought they might come back lookin' for me."

Both Trevor and Jaris had the same thought. But neither of the friends could say what they were thinking. Then Trevor spoke in a sad tone. "She turned on me, Jaris. She wouldna cared if Bo killed me."

"Stay there, Trevor," Jaris commanded. "Just stay there. We're on our way, man."

Jaris ran for his Honda, and the others followed. As Jaris got into the car and buckled up, he called Mickey Jenkins.

"Mrs. Jenkins," he said. "Trevor's okay. We're bringing him home. We're on our way."

Mickey Jenkins screamed.

"Mrs. Jenkins," Jaris assured her, "I have to get going. We'll explain when we get there."

Then Jaris made a quick call to his family. He assured Mom that he was fine and all was well.

The caravan of cars and Kevin's motorcycle headed out. As they turned onto Pequot Street, Trevor was standing with Shadrach at the top of the ravine. Trevor looked pretty bad, but he was not seriously hurt. He had a swollen cheek and a purple bruise around his eye. A red scab was on his upper lip.

Jaris was the first to reach them. He held out his hand as he stepped toward Shadrach. "Thanks, man!" he said heartily.

Jaris grabbed Trevor for a long minute. The boys clung to one another, both of them crying. Then Trevor climbed into Jaris's car, and they headed for the Jenkins house. Everyone else followed in a happy convoy.

Mickey Jenkins had let Tommy know. He was in the front yard when the others pulled in. By the time everyone parked, the front yard of the small house was filled with cars. Trevor looked wide-eyed at all the vehicles. "Man!" he declared. "You'd think I was somebody important."

"You are, man!" Jaris responded, his eyes still wet from crying. "You're our friend."

Mickey Jenkins came flying from the house, her arms outstretched. She didn't look right or left. She ran to Trevor and gathered him in her arms. "My baby! My baby!" she sobbed. "Oh, Trevor, I about died."

Then Mrs. Jenkins held her son at arm's length. "You're all beat up! You're not in trouble, are you, baby?"

"No, Ma," Trevor answered. He glanced over his mother's shoulder at Jaris. "I got a lotta good friends, Ma. They tried to tell me stuff I didn't want to hear. I had to learn the hard way. Vanessa, she just wanted money. That's all she wanted from me."

"But how'd you get all beat up," Ma asked.

Trevor dropped his head. Jaris though maybe he was ashamed. Or maybe he was tired and hurting. "Friday night, we were hangin' around Pequot Street. They told me what they wanted to do—rob a house on Apache. I said no. They kept pressin' me. Bo, he had a gun. He said they weren't gonna let me go till I agreed to go with them. Finally, I said I wouldn't. I told 'em they could kill me before I'd do something so bad."

Mrs. Jenkins took her son into her arms again. "I'm just so glad you're home," she whispered. This time, Trevor held his mom at arm's length.

"Ma," he told her, "you taught me good. You can't steal from folks, go in their house, and take their stuff. That's what I told 'em. They laughed at me. Then Bo flashed his gun. Ma, I thought it was all over for me. I was shakin'. But he didn't shoot. Maybe he was afraid the gunshots would attract attention. Maybe he just

184

couldn't do it. He hit me with the gun. Then me and Bo fought. I rolled down the ravine and took off in the dark. He didn't run after me. He mighta even thought he killed me."

Trevor looked at his mother. "I didn't know what to do after that, Ma," he told her. "I had some money in my pocket. Friday night was payday. I got my face fixed up in the restroom at the twenty-four-seven. Been driftin' around the last coupla days. Eatin' junk food. Sleepin' in the ravine."

All of Alonee's posse circled around Trevor, giving him hugs. Even Kevin, who wasn't very sentimental, hugged Trevor. Kevin said Trev better get back to running track. Marko Lane was back in action, and no way should he be allowed to be the fastest man at Tubman High.

Tommy Jenkins hugged his brother too. But Jaris heard him whisper to Trevor that later on he would strangle him.

The group broke up, and the front yard emptied out. Jaris, the last to leave, gave Trevor the last hug of the night. He embraced his friend so hard Trevor couldn't breathe for a moment.

When Jaris got home, the whole family was still up. They were waiting for the lights from Jaris's car to come streaming in the window. The family poured out the front door and cheered as came up the driveway. They were having a little fun with him. But they *were* happy to see him home in one piece.

CHAPTER TEN

At school the next day, Falisha Colbert wondered what her mother had told Shadrach when they broke up. Did she tell the man that Falisha didn't like him? Falisha thought her mother had probably told him the truth, and that *was* the truth. Still, Falisha felt a little nervous because she had to see Shadrach three times a week for tutoring. With his tutoring, Falisha's grade in algebra had gone from an F to a C-plus. Chelsea had earned a B on Mr. Tidwell's last test, and she gave Shadrach the credit. Now, finally, she understood a lot about algebra.

Outside math class, Chelsea cried, "Oh, Falisha, I'm not flunking anymore. And I owe it all to Shadrach. He makes all that awful algebra so clear. He's a genius!"

"Yeah," Falisha agreed. "I used to dread going to Mr. Tidwell's class 'cause it was all Greek to me. Now I'm not so scared of algebra. You know what, though, Chelsea? I think my mom told Shadrach she couldn't be friends with him anymore 'cause of me. It's okay if she did that 'cause it's true, but I feel funny now going in and having him tutor me. I mean, he likes Mom, and now he knows I spoiled it all for him. I bet he's mad at me, and he won't want to help me anymore. I feel weird facing him. I bet he hates me."

Chelsea looked at her friend. "Shadrach doesn't hate anybody," she told her friend. "He's too good a person to hate. I asked him once if he hated those guys who planted that IED. That was what blew up and took his eye out and scarred him and stuff. He just said he didn't hate them 'cause they didn't know what they were doing."

"That's crazy!" Falisha exclaimed. "If somebody hurt me that bad, I'd hate them forever."

"Falisha," Chelsea replied, "I sorta would too. But wars are really hard to figure out sometimes. People are supposed to hurt and kill other people. Then they get to be heroes. And lotsa people hate all the time. But there are some special people who just won't hate, no matter what."

The girls started walking to their next class.

"Shadrach's like that," Chelsea went on. "I think Shadrach and people like him got so much love in them, that there's no room for hate. I've seen Shadrach with these really tiny baby opossums. He's so gentle and careful not to hurt them. I mean, I admire him so much. I admire him more than any teacher I ever had. I mean, in first grade I had Ms. Finch. I loved her and I admired her, but I admire Shadrach even more."

Falisha was still reluctant to go to Shadrach's tutoring class after school. But

Chelsea took her hand and dragged her along. All during the class, Falisha stole nervous glances at Shadrach. She thought she might catch him looking at her angrily. She imagined him thinking, "There sits that little witch who broke me up with my girl-friend." But every time Falisha met Shadrach's gaze, he looked as pleasant as he always did. Falisha thought he must be very good at hiding what he really felt. In Falisha's mind, he *had* to be really mad at her.

Falisha felt a tiny bit sad that things had all worked out as they had. She was sorry that she disliked Shadrach so much that she didn't want him in her life. Falisha hadn't wanted to be mean and to hurt anybody. But she really didn't want a stepfather, especially Shadrach. So, fighting back her shyness, Falisha spoke to Shadrach after the tutoring class was over for the day. "Mr. Shadrach, you've really helped me a lot with algebra. I didn't understand at all what Mr. Tidwell was talking about, and now I sorta do."

Shadrach smiled and replied, "Thank you for telling me, Falisha. I'm glad I can help out."

As Falisha and Chelsea were leaving the tutoring class, they ran into Kanika. She grinned at them and, as usual, had something mean to say. "I'm glad I'm smart enough so I don't have to do remedial! Especially with a scary-looking guy like Mr. Shadrach!"

Chelsea was still thinking of a comeback when Falisha surprised her by speaking in a matter-of-fact voice. "Mr. Shadrach isn't scary-looking."

Chelsea looked at Falisha but said nothing. Then Chelsea hustled to the parking lot to go home with Jaris.

"I'm sorry you gotta wait an hour longer, Jaris, 'cause of my tutoring class," Chelsea told him, as she neared the car. "But it's helping me so much."

Jaris smiled. He was at peace with the world since all was well again with Trevor. He had his friend back. "It's okay, chili pepper," he responded amiably.

"You seem really happy, Jare," Chelsea remarked, climbing in beside him and buckling up.

"I put some great new music on my iPod," Jaris explained. "Pop tried to get me interested in the blues when I was younger, but I liked rock and rap too much. Now I'm getting to like the blues and funk. There's this chick from the delta who sings great blues. I even like the old stuff—BB King, Pinetop Perkins, Honeyboy Edwards. Man, it's cool."

Chelsea grinned. "Is that why you look so happy—'cause you're listening to Honeyboy Edwards?" she asked.

"No, chili pepper, that's only a small part of it," Jaris admitted. "Trevor made it through a bad patch. He's going back on the track team. He's cutting back his hours at the Chicken Shack. He's gonna get focused again on schoolwork. He's gonna be okay. You don't know what that means to me."

"Does he miss Vanessa?" Chelsea asked.

"I'm not sure how he's feeling about that," Jaris confessed. "I think he misses the chick he thought she was. But now he knows that that chick never existed. Trevor had a kind of aha moment. When Bo was bashing in Trevor's face, she just stood there and didn't try to help at all."

Jaris was quiet. Chelsea could tell something was on his mind. "You know, Chelsea," he said after a few minutes, "I read a biography of Harriet Tubman. She had this husband she really loved. She'd been away from him for a while, and she was really excited to be with him again. She even bought him a new suit as a gift for their reunion. But then he turned his back on her. She said that, at that moment, her husband just dropped out of her heart. I think that's what happened with Trevor. Vanessa just dropped out of his heart. For good."

"I'm glad," Chelsea declared.

Ms. Colbert sometimes took in a movie on Wednesday nights. At those times,

Falisha's grandmother would come to be with her. Grandma always brought some home-baked chocolate chip cookies. She and Falisha worked a jigsaw puzzle. But this Wednesday would be the first time Mom wasn't going out.

"Grandma not coming tonight, huh Mom?" Falisha asked.

"No honey," Mom replied, "it's just us tonight." Mom smiled and added, "I've got a lot of homework to check over, and I thought I'd stay in."

For a long time, Falisha had known that her mother was going out with Shadrach on Wednesdays. They'd see a movie and stop for something to eat. Falisha could tell that her mother really enjoyed those dates. On Wednesday afternoon she'd get ready, taking a little longer with her makeup. She'd stand before the mirror and apply her lipstick very carefully. She'd put hair spray on her fluffy hair. Then she'd choose an extra special outfit, like a pretty top and jeans that looked really good on her.

She did all that for Shadrach. And watching her mom always angered Falisha. It was just more proof that Mom and Shadrach were getting closer and closer. Eventually they would want to get married. Then Falisha's whole life would be turned upside down.

Tonight, her mother was sitting on the sofa, going over science tests. She was in her frumpy old top and shapeless jeans, with no lipstick on. Falisha looked at her and felt sad. She had taken something away from her mother, something that made her happy. Falisha hadn't wanted to do that. She just didn't want to lose her mom. She thought she would if she married Shadrach. Falisha began to see that how Shadrach looked wasn't what bothered her. Just as Chelsea had predicted, the patch on his eye and the scars seemed sort of ordinary now. The real trouble was that Falisha just didn't want her life to change.

Falisha glanced at her mother from time to time. The more she looked at Mom, the sadder she felt. Mom had stopped seeing Shadrach out of love for her daughter.

Falisha was just amazed that Mom loved her so much that she would give up something so important to her.

"Mom," Falisha announced, "it would be all right if you still sometimes went to the movies." She didn't want to come right out and say "with him." Falisha wasn't yet ready to admit that maybe there *was* a place for Shadrach in their lives.

"I'll be going again," Mom responded.

"I bet Grandma missed coming over," Falisha suggested.

"She loves being with you, Falisha," Mom replied.

"Maybe, you know, next week, Grandma could come over," Falisha suggested. "We could start putting our new jigsaw puzzle together. Our new one is the Golden Gate Bridge."

Mom looked up. She smiled at Falisha but said nothing.

Jaris was expecting this trip to the mall with Chelsea and her friends on Friday afternoon. It was inevitable once all the stores came out with the news of "drastic price cuts." Jaris hoped it would be just Chelsea and Athena or, at the most, Chelsea, Athena, and Falisha. He wasn't at all prepared to see Chelsea, Falisha, Athena, Keisha, and Inessa all piling into his Honda Civic. As he turned the car onto the freeway, the noise level was deafening.

"There are so many cute new tops, and they're all on sale!" Keisha screamed.

"Jaris, you're going so slow," Chelsea scolded. "Look, all the other cars are passing us. You drive like Grandma!"

"So be it," Jaris declared, not driving one bit faster. He had precious cargo aboard.

When they got to the store, the five girls all rushed off in different directions. Only Inessa was looking at the reasonably decent clothes. Jaris was keeping a close eye on Chelsea. Pop was more concerned than ever about how she dressed since his mechanic mistook her for a "hot chick."

"Look!" Falisha screamed from the far end of the racks. The others rushed to join her. She'd found the mother lode of tops.

"Oh, is that ever cute?" Chelsea chirped, grabbing a pink top.

Falisha held a sea green graphic knit top with the likeness of an animal on it. It looked like an opossum, pouch and all. The message was, "There's room for you too." Falisha lifted the top off the hanger. "It's my size," she noted with a sense of awe. "And there's just one."

The other girls looked at one another but said nothing. "I like it," Falisha announced. "Do you guys like it?"

"It's you, Falisha," Chelsea said. "That color is just amazing for you."

"It's fabulous, Falisha," Athena added.

On Monday, Mr. Tidwell gave a hard class in algebra. Even the good students struggled. Chelsea and Falisha were completely confused. More kids from Mr. Tidwell's class had signed up for tutoring with

Shadrach. They had to move his class to a bigger room right off the library.

When Shadrach saw the army of kids coming, he brought out more chairs and desks.

"Come on, you guys!" he urged. "Time to conquer old devil algebra. He thinks he's got you, but we know better." When Falisha entered the room, Shadrach did a double take. She was wearing her new top. It looked pretty, but that's not what caught his eye.

When the tutoring session ended, Chelsea and Falisha were the last students in the room. Chelsea went outside, but Falisha remained. Chelsea knew Falisha wanted to say something to Shadrach.

Falisha walked up to Shadrach's desk and stood there in her green top. The top bore the likeness of an opossum, though it was cartoony enough maybe to be something else. Clear to see was the opossum's pouch, with a baby opossum peeking out of it. Above the image were the words, "There's room for you too."

"Cute top, Falisha," Shadrach noted.

"Yeah. I just got it," Falisha replied. "There was only one like it."

Shadrach nodded. He didn't say anything.

"I miss them too," Falisha remarked.

"What do you miss, Falisha?" Shadrach asked.

"Wednesdays," the girl responded. "Grandma always came. We had chocolate chip cookies, and we did jigsaw puzzles. Mom misses her Wednesdays too. The movies and stuff."

"I miss them too," Shadrach said.

"So I guess maybe you should go to the movies with Mom again?" Falisha suggested.

Falisha couldn't come right out and say what she felt. She was naturally shy, and, anyway, this conversation was very hard. She had seen Shadrach as the one Mom loved more than her. Now she knew that wasn't true. Mom loved her the best, and that was all that she needed to know.

Everything Falisha wanted to say was right there on her top: "There's room for you too."

"You're nice," Falisha remarked, turning quickly and running to join Chelsea outside.

Shadrach came to the door of the tutoring room. He stood there talking on his cell phone.

Chelsea grabbed Falisha's hand and whispered, "He's callin' your mom I bet."

Falisha giggled a little. "I gotta call Grandma," she said.

The girls hugged each other parted. Falisha started home. Chelsea ran toward Jaris, who was leaning on his car.

During the drive home, Jaris was quieter than usual.

"Whatcha thinking about, Jare?" Chelsea asked.

"Well, chili pepper," he responded, "it's been crazy the last week or so. Hasn't it?"

Chelsea nodded yes but said nothing.

Jaris went on. "I mean, Trevor did some nutty things out of love for Vanessa. And she didn't care a bit about him. Tommy loves Trevor. But he had to get tough with him to get him back on track."

Jaris reflected for a second or two. "Falisha's mom," he continued, "she loves Shadrach. But she was ready to give him up out of love for her daughter. Then Falisha saw how much her mom was hurting. She made room in her heart for Shadrach. And she did that out of love for her mother."

Chelsea was listening all the while. Finally, she made a comment. "Man, we do all kinds of things out of love for someone else. Don't we, Jare?"